D1713788

Romance at the Hacienda

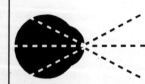 This Large Print Book carries the
Seal of Approval of N.A.V.H.

ROMANCE AT THE HACIENDA

COLLEEN L. REECE

THORNDIKE PRESS
A part of Gale, Cengage Learning

GALE
CENGAGE Learning·

Detroit • New York • San Francisco • New Haven, Conn • Waterville, Maine • London

GALE
CENGAGE Learning

Copyright © 2012 by Colleen L. Reece.
All scripture quotations are taken from the King James Version of the Bible.
Thorndike Press, a part of Gale, Cengage Learning.

ALL RIGHTS RESERVED
All of the characters and events in this book are fictitious. Any resemblance to actual persons, living or dead, or to actual events is purely coincidental.
Thorndike Press® Large Print Christian Romance.
The text of this Large Print edition is unabridged.
Other aspects of the book may vary from the original edition.
Set in 16 pt. Plantin.

LIBRARY OF CONGRESS CATALOGING-IN-PUBLICATION DATA

Reece, Colleen L.
   Romance at the hacienda / by Colleen L. Reece.
      pages ; cm. — (Thorndike Press large print Christian romance)
    ISBN 978-1-4104-5859-9 (hardcover) — ISBN 1-4104-5859-8 (hardcover) 1.
   Large type books. I. Title.
   PS3568.E3646R66 2013
   813'.54—dc23   2013004463

Published in 2013 by arrangement with Barbour Publishing, Inc.

Printed in Mexico
1 2 3 4 5 6 7 17 16 15 14 13

For my faithful fans
who always want more . . .

A NOTE FROM THE AUTHOR

I love to hear from my readers! You may correspond with me by writing:

Colleen L. Reece
Author Relations
PO Box 721
Uhrichsville, OH 44683

ONE

San Francisco
June 16, 1896

Heedless of the moisture-laden breeze that billowed the draperies and her fragile white dress, Angel Montoya clutched the iron grillwork outside her bedroom window. Tear-drenched eyes stared at the Pacific Ocean that seemed to stretch on forever. Snatches of the heartrending news that had rocked the world churned in her mind:

June 15. Most devastating tsunami in Japanese history. Generated by 8.5 magnitude earthquake off coast of Sanriku. Height, 25 meters (80 feet). Swept away all houses and people when it reached land. At least 22,000 deaths.

Observed across the Pacific. Wharves in Hawaii demolished. Houses swept away. *San Francisco Chronicle* reports 9.5 foot wave observed along California Coast.

A drift of laughter rose from the courtyard three stories below. Filled with revulsion at the sound, Angel covered her ears. How could people laugh when cries of despair echoed from thousands of miles across the cruel sea? Families desperately seeking loved ones. Fishermen, twenty miles out to sea, hadn't noticed the wave beneath their boats; it had only been fifteen inches high at the time.

Angel shuddered. What had those men felt when they returned to Sanriku? Devastation. Thousands gone in the twinkling of an eye, and 170 miles of coastline destroyed!

"Where was *Dios*?" Angel whispered. "All those people —"

The heavy bedroom door flew open and cut short her prayer. An outraged gasp followed. "Angelina Carmencita Olivera Montoya, what are you doing?"

Eyes as black as Guadalupe Garcia's mantilla and costly lace gown sparked with anger. She sniffed, sailed to the window, and slammed it shut. Then she caught Angel by the shoulder and whirled her toward an ornately framed mirror. "Look at yourself."

Angel stared at her once-exquisite gown. The tiers of fine lace hung limp and dejected. "I'm sorry, *Tía.*"

"Your dress is ruined. How could you?"

10

Guadalupe released Angel, flung open the carved doors of an enormous wardrobe, and sniffed again. "I don't know what you are going to wear. Some of your guests have seen all your other gowns."

Angel held back the words: *Not my guests. Yours.* Twelve years in Tía Guadalupe and Tío Miguel's care had taught her the folly of answering back. "I truly am sorry, but" — a sob escaped — "what difference does it make when so many people have lost their homes and families and lives?"

Guadalupe gaped then drew herself to her full five-foot height. "What *difference*? Feeling sorry for the misfortunes of others is all well and good, Angelina. But we must carry on. After all, we owe a great deal to those who have come to honor you on your eighteenth birthday."

She pawed through the array of stunning gowns. "Besides, don't you want your last night in San Francisco to be unforgettable?" Her eyes grew moist. "If only my brother-in-law hadn't insisted . . ." Guadalupe sighed and snatched a rose-pink gown from the wardrobe. "This will do." She thrust the dress at Angel. "You'll have to manage on your own. The servants are all busy elsewhere."

The great door swung shut behind her

11

aunt, but her words lingered in the air. Angel automatically finished her aunt's complaint, as she had done countless times before: "If only your father had not stipulated that once you reached eighteen you must return to *La Casa del Sol.*" Despite the need for haste, Angel remained standing at the mirror, lost in the past. . . .

She had been only six years old when her mother had died giving birth to the son Don Fernando waited for after his girl-child was born. Angel remembered her father scooping her up in his strong arms. She had never seen him cry, but tears flowed when he said, "*Mamá* and your brother have gone to heaven, Angelina. I cannot take proper care of a little girl. Tía Guadalupe and Tío Miguel have no children. They love you very much. They will take you to San Francisco and care for you until you are eighteen. Then you will come home to me."

"I don't want to leave the hacienda," Angel wailed.

"You must be brave, *niñita.* I shall come see you when I can. Do what you are told, and one day we shall be together again," Don Fernando promised.

Angel's aunt and uncle never knew that their niece cried herself to sleep for days before resigning herself to following her father's command and counting the weeks, months, and years before she would be free. She tried hard to please Guadalupe and the nuns at the convent, where she was sent to school. Yet with each passing year, the pretentious Garcia mansion felt less like home. Angel longed for La Casa del Sol, the house of the sun. Perhaps there she could be free of the restrictions and expectations placed on her because of the Garcias' high position in Spanish society.

Now Angel smiled. There had been some special times to brighten her sheltered life. Especially her *quinceañera.* How handsome *Papá* had looked when he escorted her to the table, which held fifteen lighted candles in honor of his daughter having accomplished that many years. Taller than many men of his position, straight as an oak, he showed every bit of his Spanish-grandee heritage.

The best part of the celebration was when he sighed and whispered, "Just three more years."

"Do you miss me, Papá?"

"More than life itself." He caught her in a fierce embrace. "If I had not given my word, I would spirit you away this very night. It cannot be. A man who breaks his word is no better than a serpent that crawls on the

13

ground."

His statement effectively silenced Angel's desire to beg him to take her home.

A knock on the door roused Angel from her trip into the past. *"Adelante!"*

The door opened, and an anxious face peered in. "Senora Garcia says you must come now." Conchita, more companion to Angel than servant, clapped her hands. A warm smile lit up her face. "Senorita, you are beautiful!" She wrinkled her forehead. "But where is the white dress you planned to wear?"

Angel pointed to the damp, crumpled gown that lay where she had stepped out of it. "Tía Guadalupe is not happy with me."

Conchita picked up the dress and wrinkled her nose. "It smells like the sea. You have been standing by the open window again, *sí*?" She folded the once-pristine gown and looked solemn. "I cannot believe you are really leaving us tomorrow."

Angel secured the last closure in the row of buttons that marched from her waist to the modest neckline of her gown and smoothed down a lace-edged ruffle. A thrill of anticipation surged through her. "Yes. I am going home with my father."

Tears welled in Conchita's dark eyes. "I

14

shall miss you." She hesitated then blurted out, "Will you take a *duenna* with you?"

Angel laughed. "I don't know why I would need a chaperone on the hacienda. Surely life there will not be as formal as here." She tilted her head to one side and secured her white lace mantilla more firmly. The pain in Conchita's face reflected next to her mirrored image. Suddenly, an idea burst like skyrockets over San Francisco Bay. Angel whirled and grabbed Conchita by the shoulders. "If Papá can arrange it, will you go with me?"

The little maid's mouth dropped open. "I? Go to La Casa del Sol?"

"Why not? Tía Guadalupe has many servants. She doesn't need you, and you have no family." A lump came to Angel's throat. "I need you, Conchita. Not as a servant but as a friend and companion." Memories of secret hours spent together sharing like two ordinary girls not irrevocably separated by the caste system flooded Angel. "You have been my *hermanita,* the little sister I never had."

The joy in Conchita's face more than repaid Angel. Two strong hands grabbed her and hugged her so hard Angel protested, "Mercy, don't squeeze the life out of me!"

"I cannot help myself." Conchita's face

clouded, and her hands dropped. "What if Don Fernando cannot convince the Garcias to let me go?"

"He can talk the birds out of the trees," Angel told her. She hurried to a nearby desk, took out writing materials, and hastily scribbled,

I must see you before I come down.

She folded the page, thrust it into Conchita's hands, and pushed her toward the door. "Take this to my father."

Conchita looked uncertain.

"Go!" Angel ordered with a laugh.

Conchita vanished.

The closing of the door brought Angel to her senses. Remorse filled her. What had she done? Why hadn't she asked her father before tantalizing Conchita with a future that might not be? Bowing her head, Angel prayed, "*Por favor,* Dios, open the way for Conchita to go with me."

The time between the sending of the note and her father's appearance felt like years. When he stepped into Angel's room, a worry line was etched between his black brows. "What is the matter, *querida*? Surely you are not ill!"

"No. Oh, no." She ran to him. "I just needed to see you."

A white smile gleamed beneath his small,

16

dark mustache, and he opened his arms wide. "You could not wait until you came downstairs?"

"No!" She laughed and threw her arms around him. "I could not wait even one minute longer." She buried her face against his heavily embroidered waistcoat and clung to him.

"Querida, beloved, you need wait no more. Tomorrow we go home." Infinite gentleness underscored each word.

"That is why I had to see you now." Angel tipped her head back and looked into his eyes. "Can you arrange for us to take Conchita? I will miss her so much."

"Then she must go with us. But pray tell, what is Conchita? A horse? A dog?"

Laughter bubbled up inside Angel and spilled out. "No. Conchita is the servant who brought you my note. She is my best friend."

"Ah," he teased, "I was not so far off thinking she is an animal. She scuttled up to me like a frightened rabbit."

Angel couldn't help laughing again. "She's a girl just like me, except a few months younger. I cannot bear for us to be parted."

He smiled. "I will arrange it. Your aunt will surely be pleased knowing a servant she has trained so well is to be your companion."

He sighed, but the twinkle in his eyes betrayed him when he said, "Oh dear, now I will have two young ladies on my hands instead of one. Never mind. Never let it be said that the *hacendado* of La Casa del Sol was defeated by two young girls. Now, we had best get downstairs before Guadalupe summons half the San Francisco police force to search for us." He bowed and offered his arm.

Angel slipped on her lace mitts, took up a stiff lace fan, and tucked one hand through the curve of her father's elbow. On a wave of happiness, she descended the stairs to the party for both celebrating her birthday and saying farewell. Catching sight of Conchita at the bottom of the last flight of stairs, she smiled and gave a quick nod. The flare of understanding in the other girl's face lighted a candle of joy in Angel's heart. She felt it glow throughout the long hours of feasting and merriment that followed.

Most of the guests lingered until the wee hours of the morning, but at last they departed. The strum of guitars in a farewell serenade outside Angel's window ceased. Only the distant moaning of the ocean's restless waters and a foghorn warning ships to beware broke the silence. Alone in the bedroom, Angel and Conchita rejoiced that the Garcias had released Conchita from service, but the girls were too excited to sleep.

"Did you have a chance to pack?" Angel asked.

"It did not take long." Conchita giggled and looked at Angel's mountain of baggage awaiting departure. "I hope the ferry does not sink from all your bags and boxes when we cross the bay in the morning."

"We will pray that it does not." Angel sobered. "Conchita, we must also pray for the families of those lost in Japan. And those whose homes the sea swallowed." Tears she had willed to stay back during the party burned behind her eyelids.

Conchita's giggle died. "It is a terrible thing."

"I do not understand how a loving God can allow such things," Angel cried.

Conchita's dark, troubled eyes took on a faraway look. "I do not know, senorita. I have asked Dios that many times."

Angel held her breath. Would Conchita's next words help to resolve the questions about God that haunted Angel? Or were there no answers?

Conchita laid her hand on Angel's arm. A

look of peace stole into her eyes. "I have come to believe that I do not have to know why things happen. I am only a servant girl, not Dios. All I need to do is to trust Him."

After Conchita went to her room, Angel knelt and prayed, "Is this the answer when there seem to be no answers? Just to trust and accept that I don't always need to understand? It sounds too simple."

Angel's heart still ached for those who had lost so much, but she finally managed to fall asleep. When she awoke, Conchita was opening the draperies to a sun-splashed morning . . . and wearing a smile as brilliant as the first day of their new life.

TWO

Angelina clasped her gloved hands on the
ferryboat rail and watched the San Francisco skyline dwindle in the distance. The
beat of her heart kept time with the chug-
ging of the engine.

"Any regrets?" her father asked.

"Just that Tía Guadalupe never let me ride
the cable cars. She said it was too dangerous." Angel surreptitiously squeezed Conchita's arm and was rewarded with a giggle.
Then a shout of laughter from her father
made her wonder if she should have remained silent. "Sorry, Papá. Tía and Tío
were good to me."

"Why did you not tell me you wished to
ride the cars?" He smiled at her. "I myself
would have taken you."

Angel's eyes opened wide in astonishment.

"Sí." He waved a careless hand toward the
city. "But no matter. There are far better

things than cable cars at La Casa del Sol."

She linked arms with him. "Why do you sound so mysterious?"

"You will find out soon," he teased. "Not now. Querida, will you not miss the city at all?"

"I never was able to see much of it," she confessed. "My lessons took a great deal of time. I also had to practice on the piano and the guitar. We had much company, and Tía always wanted me to play for them."

"Poor little cooped-up bird." Papá patted her hand. "Now you are ready to try your wings. Just do not fly away from me." A broad smile appeared. "Speaking of birds and music, I seem to remember that the Garcias took you to hear the Sierra Songbird when she was in San Francisco a few years ago."

A thrill went through Angel. "Sí. I never heard a voice like Senorita Sterling's, even though I only heard her once. The *San Francisco Chronicle* reported that she gave up her career to get married."

Papá chuckled. "The report was correct. She often sings in the church at Madera. Her husband is the pastor."

Conchita gasped, and Angel's heart pounded. "Then I — we — will meet her?"

He knitted his brows. "Oh yes. The couple

has an interesting story. Joshua Stanhope is the son of a wealthy San Francisco family. He walked away from fame and fortune at a large church there and came to Madera. He met and married Senorita Ellianna Sterling, the Sierra Songbird."

"What made him do it?"

Her father looked solemn, and an unreadable expression crept into his eyes. "Senor Stanhope felt it was what God wanted him to do." He paused then added, "One must always do what He asks. Angelina, there is something I must tell you."

"Do you want me to go away, senor?" Conchita quavered.

"Stay, por favor. I want you to hear this."

Something in her father's manner sent fear through Angel. She exchanged puzzled glances with Conchita but received no enlightenment. Her mind raced. Why did he, bravest of the brave, hesitate to speak? She had done nothing to incur his displeasure. Angel racked her brain trying to think what could have changed him. She knew of no crop failures or the loss of cattle.

A horrid thought slid into her mind. *What if after all these years alone, Papá has met someone and decided to marry again?*

Angel shivered and pulled her traveling cloak closer. *Surely not,* her heart protested.

Not when I am just now coming home. If he were to be wed, he would have told me. She tightened her grip on his arm. After all the years away from her father, must she now share him with another?

He gently freed himself and placed both hands on her shoulders. "Querida, this will come as a shock, but" — he took a deep breath and slowly released it — "strange things have been happening. They trouble me." His voice dwindled to a whisper. "I sometimes find myself questioning what I have always believed, and asking if Dios cares about me."

Conchita's fingers dug into Angel's arm, but she barely felt them. Her heart skipped a beat, then raced. This could not be. Her father had studied for the priesthood until he met and married lovely Carmencita Olivera after a whirlwind courtship. Even then, he had remained true to his childhood teachings. Mass was observed daily in the chapel at La Casa del Sol.

Memories crowded into Angel's throbbing heart: the deep-toned bell that summoned the faithful to worship; Father Alfonso and the altar boys; rows of kneeling *peones* and *vaqueros*. Most of all, she remembered how hundreds of flickering candles brought the stained-glass windows to life.

Angel shivered, chilled more by her father's statement than the mist rising from the bay. How could Papá question the teachings of the church? The pageantry of fast and feast days? The Holy Communion? What would Tía and Tío say? That he was no longer a fit parent for their niece? She tried to speak. No words came.

Her father's hands fell from Angel's shoulders. "Come." He led his daughter and a frightened-looking Conchita inside and seated them at a distance from the other passengers. "When your Mamá and little brother died, I was blinded by loss. I foolishly listened to Guadalupe and Miguel's pleas to take you. A thousand times I regretted it but . . ." His face turned somber. "I had given my word."

Angel wanted to cry out how much she wished he had kept her with him, but she could not speak in the face of such regret.

Her father turned and looked out across the water. "I could not understand why we were left alone. I stormed heaven, asking for answers. There were none, at least none that I could find."

Angel flinched from the pain in his voice and clenched her hands until the nails bit into her palms. Had she not done the same thing only the night before?

He went on. "Weeks turned into years. Neighbors were kind, especially the Sterlings and Andersons from the Diamond S. I remained frozen. The only thing that saved my sanity was knowing this day would come. When you returned home, I would again know peace. I clung to the thought like a drowning man clings to a plank. Each time I visited San Francisco, I fought the growing temptation to take you home. Pride in keeping my word prevented it."

He turned back to her as if returning from a long journey. "One day a rider came to the hacienda: Senor Red Fallon, a ruffian who had been driven from the San Joaquin Valley years before. I wondered why such a man should come to La Casa del Sol. He asked permission to water his horse. I could not refuse such a request, for the beast stood with drooping head, and the man's dusty clothing showed they had come a long distance.

" 'Water him and go,' I commanded.

"Senor Fallon doffed his worn sombrero. '*Gracias*. May I, too, drink?'

"I nodded, wishing they would leave without knowing why. Something about the unannounced visitor disturbed me. But I could not help noticing how thoroughly he cared for his horse, as if they were *com-*

26

pañeros who had ridden many trails together. Only after the horse had taken his fill did his master quench his own thirst. Then he looked deep into my eyes and said, 'Senor Montoya, I have a message for you. God loves you. He offers you peace.'

"Black anger rose within me. 'If Dios has a message for me, why would he send it by you, senor?' I challenged, remembering the hours I had spent seeking peace and finding none. Was this ragtag range rider *loco*? I opened my mouth to order him off the hacienda but was struck dumb by his next words.

" 'Senor. We have both been without hope. God had mercy on me. He longs to do the same for you.'

"When I could finally get words out of my constricted throat, I thundered, 'How dare you compare your miserable self to a Montoya?' Yet something prevented me from having the presumptuous rider thrown off the hacienda." Papá passed a shaking hand over his eyes as if to clear his vision.

Angel's heart beat like a gong, and she leaned forward. She felt Conchita move closer to her and welcomed the warmth of the other girl's body. "What happened?"

Her father stroked his mustache. "Even now I can scarcely believe it, but I permit-

27

ted Fallon to tell me what happened to him after he left Madera. He drifted west and ended up beaten almost to death in a back alley of San Francisco. A young man rescued him and took him to a mission. Workers there cared for him, and his life changed through what he called 'soup, soap, and salvation.' When well enough to travel, he returned to Madera, did his best to undo the harm he had done, and began telling his story. The former *bandido* was also the means of bringing Pastor Josh Stanhope to Madera."

Angel struggled to understand. "Why should this affect you?"

He grimaced. "I could not get Senor Fallon's story out of my mind. In spite of his rough clothing and ways, he wore peace like a cloak. Peace I desperately needed and had not found — although I had lighted hundreds of candles, given generously to the church, confessed my sins to Father Alfonso, and fasted again and again." He clenched his hands into fists. "Why should something I needed so badly be given to such a one as Senor Fallon and not to me?"

Angel swallowed hard and laid her hands over her father's. "I do not know."

"Nor do I." His hands relaxed and gently covered hers. His sigh sounded as if it started at the toes of his hand-tooled boots and moved upward. "I also do not understand why the memory of Senor Fallon's face rode with me for weeks. Or why he came long miles to tell me God loved me and offered peace." His face darkened. "I had long since begun to believe there is no peace. Just heartache and struggle."

Angel felt tears spring to her eyes. "Please, Papá, you must not say that!"

"Forgive me. I should not afflict you. Or you, Conchita." A smile bloomed. "What kind of welcome to the hacienda is it for me to burden you with my doubts and troubles? Let us forget them and be joyous."

"Your troubles are also mine," Angel cried.

"And mine," Conchita whispered.

The tenderness in his gaze did not dispel Angel's feelings that he was holding something back. "Is there something more?"

"Sí." He brought her clasped hands to his breast. "Just when I thought myself free from memories of Senor Fallon's visit, another strange thing happened. One morning in Madera, I heard singing pouring through the open windows of the church. I recognized the Sierra Songbird's voice, singing as I had never heard anyone sing. I had ridden past the church countless times and heard other songs, but that day the words caused me to stop. The notes came as a shower of gold." He drew in a ragged breath and sang:

" 'Peace, peace, wonderful peace,
    Coming down from the Father above!
Sweep over my spirit forever, I pray
    In fathomless billows of love!'

"I goaded my stallion into a run and cried to the heavens that had shut themselves to me when Dios took Carmencita and my son. 'Why do you withhold peace from me?' I shouted. 'What have I done to deserve such treatment?' "

Angel flung herself against him, unable to bear the sight of his face. Would Papá have suffered like this had she been with him? Would he not have been so absorbed in caring for his motherless daughter that some of the pain would have fled? Suddenly, she hated the Garcias for taking her away.

Her father's impassioned voice lowered to a whisper. "Again, there was no answer. There still is none. I call myself loco for hoping to one day find peace." He paused then added, "Yet how can a man live without hope?"

The ferryboat whistle warned they had neared their destination. It sounded like a

30

death blow to Angel's rosy dreams. If her father could not find that which he sought, dark clouds would hover over the House of the Sun.

THREE

Zing. Timothy Sterling's lasso sang through the air and settled over a bawling calf's head. He leaped from Blue's saddle and ran toward the animal struggling to free itself from a thicket.

"Stupid critter," Tim grouched. "This is what happens when you wander away from your mama." Strong gloved hands soon freed the calf, but it didn't help Tim's bad mood. Neither did the huge, black thundercloud heading his way. Thunder meant lightning even when it didn't bring rain. Tim's blue roan hated both.

An irate bellow and the sound of pounding hooves alerted Tim that Mama had discovered her darling's absence and was charging toward him like an entire regiment of cavalry. He swatted the calf's hindquarters, watched the family reunion then vaulted into the saddle. "Make tracks, Old Man. We're a long way from town and already late."

Blue responded with a leap that would have unseated a less-skilled rider. Tim let out a cowboy yell and squeezed his knees against the powerful stallion's sides. He crouched low over Blue's neck and stuck like a burr. Yet it seemed ages before they reached the road that ran from the Diamond S ranch to the parsonage in Madera.

"We'da been there by now if it hadn't been for that dumb calf," Tim complained. The next moment, thoughts of the hand-carved pony stowed in his saddlebag chased away his annoyance. "It's perfect for little Timmy's birthday," Tim told his horse, "and it will go a long way in making up for my being late to the party."

He cocked a dark eyebrow. "The sun may not rise and set with Timothy Edward Stanhope, but no one will ever convince Josh and Ellie of that." He grinned. "I have to admit: Timmy's a great little fella. He should be since he's named after me."

Blue flicked an ear and snorted but didn't break stride.

Tim's restored high spirits spilled into a laugh. "That's telling me. I'd better keep conceit to myself, right?" He let the roan run a little longer then reined him into a ground-covering lope and gloated over the nephew he adored. Small Timmy already shared his uncle's love for horses. Ever since Tim first swung the child into the saddle and let him help hold the reins, his namesake greeted him on all occasions by crying, "Up horsey, Unca Tim."

Tim relaxed in the saddle and half closed his eyes. Blue had traveled the road to town so many times that he needed no urging. The ten miles afforded Tim the opportunity for some of his best thinking. His heartbeat quickened. How different young Timmy's childhood would be from his own!

"Lord, I'm glad You finally helped heal my bitterness toward my father," Tim prayed. "And even more that Matt and Sarah adopted Ellie and me."

A picture of himself at eight, crying at the St. Louis train station and clinging to his eleven-year-old sister's bedraggled skirts, came to mind. Time had dulled the harsh edges of memory, but a wave of gratitude filled him. "Hard to believe Ellie and I were ever Stoddards. I've been a Sterling far longer than I was a Stoddard. Thanks for making it happen, God."

Tim continued to dream until Blue slackened his pace and brought him out of his woolgathering. "Here already, Old Man? Good for you." He glanced at the buggies

34

and horses in front of the parsonage next door to Christ the Way Church. "Looks like the whole clan is here. Wouldja look at all that food!"

Tim stared at the heavily laden tables and slid out of the saddle. He tossed the reins to the dusty earth. Blue had been trained to stand when ground-tied.

A small, dark-haired, brown-eyed tornado in a miniature cowboy suit tore free from his father's arms and headed for Tim. According to Tim's stepsister, Sarah, Timmy was the "spittin' image" of his uncle when he was a child. The little buckaroo's shrill cry rose above the babble of adult voices and the shouts of children playing hide-and-seek among the nearby trees.

"Up horsey, Unca Tim. Up horsey!"

Love for the little guy flooded Tim. "Later. Right now I have a present for you."

Timmy clapped his hands. His eyes shone. "A pwesent? For me?"

"You're the birthday boy, aren't you?"

"Yes!" Timmy hollered.

Tim took the painstakingly carved figurine from his saddlebag and unwrapped it. "This is your very own horse."

Chubby fingers stroked the highly polished wood. "Is that his name? Vewy Own?"

Tim smothered a chuckle and glared at

those around them when they laughed. "Why not? I reckon a man can call his horse anything he chooses."

Timmy clutched his present and ran to his mother. "See, Mama? Vewy Own."

"What do you say to Uncle Tim?" Ellie prompted. She sounded so matronly that Tim hid a grin. It was still hard for Tim to think of her as the mother of the rambunctious little boy.

"Thank you." Timmy raced back to Tim and hugged him. "Up horsey now, Unca Tim?"

"Go ahead," Ellie said. "He won't settle down until you give him a ride. We can hold dinner a few more minutes."

Tim swung the child — toy and all — into the saddle and stepped up behind him. Their closeness and the child's perfect trust made Tim vow, *If I ever have a son I hope he's just like Timmy.* Laughter bubbled in his throat. Where had that come from? He'd never met a girl he had even considered marrying — in spite of the highly praised specimens of eligible maidenhood his family paraded before him.

Tim snickered. It took some doing to avoid the traps Ellie and Sarah laid for him, but so far he'd been successful in what he considered a battle of wits and cunning.

Pastor Josh's call to dinner cut short Tim's thoughts. He halted Blue and stepped down, prying Timmy's obviously reluctant fingers from the reins and returning him to his mother. Josh asked God's blessing on the food and family and announced, "Dig in."

"Gladly." Tim's stomach rumbled. Finding that ornery calf had left no time to eat. He felt hollow from the tips of his dusty boots to the Stetson he'd removed for the blessing and tossed aside. The tantalizing aroma of fried chicken, baked beans, and enough pies and cobbler to satisfy even the hungry horde swarming to the table made his mouth water.

Conversation dwindled and died until the birthday feast ended. With a sigh of repletion, Tim stretched out on the ground and leaned back against the trunk of a nearby oak whose canopy of leaves blocked the hot sun. Could anything be more peaceful than this perfect summer day? Even the thundercloud had moved on.

Tim's sense of well-being ended when Seth dropped down beside him.

"Enjoy yourself while you can, little brother." He gave an exaggerated sigh. "Once you're married, life is never the same."

Tim sat bolt upright and stared at Seth. "Married! Me?"

Seth's eyes twinkled. "You're crowding nineteen. Time to be finding a wife."

"I agree." Matt Sterling settled on the ground next to them.

Josh looked down at the trio and chimed in. "So do I. Marriage is the best thing that can happen to a man."

Tim gulped. What had brought that up? And why now? He certainly didn't believe in mind reading. Still, it seemed strange for Seth to harp on marriage just after Tim had been congratulating himself on thwarting the women's plots!

Seth locked his hands behind his head and mused. "I can see it all now. Tim's gonna be one of those galoots who falls in love at first sight."

"When the San Joaquin River runs dry," Tim scoffed. "Love at first sight is a myth for the weak-minded to believe."

"Whoa there, boy," Matt protested. "Don't make rash statements. Your stepsister Sarah and I fell in love with each other's pictures!"

Tim felt himself redden and wished, "Uh, yeah, but —"

"But nothing," Josh inserted. "I fell in love with Ellie when she tripped and fell down at the fiesta where I first saw her. She says she did the same."

Tim wished he'd held his tongue. He turned to Seth in desperation. "You can't say you fell in love with Dori at first sight. Seems I remember every time you saw her picture you thought what a shame it was for Matt to have such a spoiled, headstrong sister."

Seth smirked. "Yeah, even though I couldn't keep from staring at Dori's picture every time I was in the ranch house!"

A shout of laughter followed, but Seth quickly added, "I have to admit, we rode some rocky trails before discovering God had planned all along for us to marry." His gaze rested on Caleb and Gideon, busy with a game of tag nearby. "I can't imagine not having those two."

Neither could Tim, but he wasn't about to admit it. "Can we talk about something else?" He stood and planted his hands on his hips. "If God wants me to get married, I guarantee it won't be by me falling in love with a picture. Or being polite enough to help up a young lady who sprawls at my feet." He glared at his tormentors and strode away, accompanied by Seth's mocking voice.

"To paraphrase the words of a certain gentleman named William Shakespeare,

'Methinks thou dost protest too much.' I can hardly wait to see what God has in store for you, little brother."

Tim was tempted to whirl on his boot heel and say he could very well wait, but he reconsidered. The chances of besting one of his relatives at a time were fair to good. Winning an argument against all three when they were united reduced the odds to zero — especially when the subject came to marriage. The wisest course was to ignore them and walk away.

Another quote came to mind: *He who fights and runs away will live to fight another day.* Tim's irritation vanished. Time would show who was right. And it wouldn't be by him falling in love at first sight.

The day sped by on winged feet. Late-afternoon shadows appeared all too soon. Timmy had long since fallen asleep curled up next to Tim on a blanket and still hanging on to "Vewy Own." Tim silently thanked God for the precious little boy and for all his family. He carried Timmy inside the parsonage, which had been expanded to accommodate the child, and tucked him into bed.

"You'll make a wonderful father," Ellie whispered from beside him.

Tim groaned. "Not you, too! Why is

everyone so bent on seeing me get hitched?"

Ellie pointed to her son. "That is one of the reasons." Love flowed from her.

Tim's heart bounced, but he merely pulled the sheet higher over Timmy's body. "I have plenty of time since I'm not a grizzled old man. How about leaving it up to God?"

"I will if you will," Ellie promised, but even in the room lit only by the sun's parting ray he could see the mischief in her face.

"It's a bargain." Tim held out his hand, and they shook on it.

Later that night riding home under the stars, Tim relived special moments of the day: Timmy snuggled in his arms, trusting him for protection. The deep devotion in the eyes of the men when they spoke of their wives. Ellie's whispered comment about Tim making a wonderful father.

A feeling of excitement washed through him. What if the next bend in the road held unsuspected treasure? He shrugged at the thought but a moment later murmured to Blue, "Old Man, I've gotta admit it's gonna be all-fired interesting to see what God has in mind!"

FOUR

The Montoyas and Conchita were barely seated in the eastbound train before the conductor bellowed a warning cry. "All abo–ard!"

Conchita gasped. Angel's heart pounded until it seemed the other travelers in the car must hear. In a few minutes she would be on her way. Away from the sheltered life she had endured without realizing until now how much she had longed for freedom. *Freedom.* A beautiful word! Angel squeezed Conchita's hand and studied the passenger coach.

Gingerbread trimmings. Polished brass lamps hanging from the ceiling. Stained-glass transoms that cast rainbow colors across the rich, plush seats.

Angel thought of the dining car she had glimpsed from the station platform before they boarded. Tablecloths as white and spotless as those used in the Garcia home. Attendants going about their duties in the same well-trained manner displayed by those who served Tía Guadalupe and Tío Miguel.

Angel turned to her father and blurted out, "Why did you always come to see me but never let me visit La Casa del Sol?"

Sadness settled over her father's face like an evening shadow, and Angel wished she had held her tongue. "I wanted to do so many times. Yet I knew in my heart if I ever brought you home I could not bear to return you, in spite of my promise. But let us talk of the future, not the past." He smiled at Conchita. "Can you ride a horse?"

She gulped and shook her head, although eagerness danced in her dark eyes. "Do you have many *caballos,* senor? I would like to ride if one is willing to carry me."

He burst out laughing. "Then we must find one among the many on the hacienda who is willing." He smiled at Angel. "What of you, niñita? Do you also need a willing horse?"

Angel thought of the riding lessons at which she had excelled and inwardly chuckled. "If Senor Horse is not willing, I shall soon make him so!" She frowned. "Papá, must I ride sidesaddle as Tía and the riding master insisted I do?"

He raised one eyebrow. "Oh, no. You shall ride as your mamá rode, astride and laughing at the wind."

Angel thrilled at the thought of galloping across the vast stretches she knew surrounded La Casa del Sol instead of being held to the sedate pace considered proper for young ladies in San Francisco. A hundred times she had longed to break free but refrained because of the consequences. Poking along with the giggling girls in her class was better than not being permitted to ride at all.

"Gracias." Angel exchanged glances with Conchita, who obviously shared her anticipation. Contentment made her say, "Oh, but I am so glad we are going home!"

A poignant light crept into Papá's eyes. "As am I." He captured Angel's hand. "Once more there will be joy in the House of the Sun."

In spite of her heart whispering *I pray it shall be so,* Angel secretly wondered. Papá had said they must put aside the past, but it didn't seem possible their future could be one of unalloyed happiness. Would her coming really make a difference? She silently vowed to do her best to erase the shadow that darkened her father's face when he was not smiling. A quick peek at Conchita assured Angel that her friend would do the same. Gratitude for his arranging her release from the Garcias showed every time the little maid looked at him. And when he shared his long and fruitless search for peace, Conchita's expressive eyes reflected pain on her new master's behalf.

Her master? Sí. Yet Papá had made no protest when Angel pleaded to bring Conchita as an *amiga,* not just a servant. Angel felt her spirits rise. How Papá had laughed at Conchita's innocent remark about wanting a willing horse! Surely her cheery countenance would help drive away whatever storm clouds lurked ahead.

Papá's voice broke into her reverie. "Angelina, Conchita, you may wish to remove your cloaks. It will take most of the day to reach Fresno."

"Why do we go to Fresno?" Angel asked. "Does not Madera come first?"

"Only on the map. The railroad does not go directly from Oakland to Madera. We will change trains at Fresno and travel north about twenty miles, less than an hour's ride." He hesitated. "Querida, what do you remember about Madera?"

Angel squeezed her eyes shut. "Yellow dust on my boots. Isn't that funny?" Conchita giggled but Angel thought hard and

45

added, "I remember a store and a nice man who gave me candy. We went there to get letters and packages from Tía and Tío on birthdays and at Christmas." Angel opened her eyes. "Is the store still there?"

"Sí. Moore's General Store and Post Office." His eyes twinkled. "Your old friend Senor Moore has not forgotten you. He inquires about you each time I go to his store."

Warmth flooded through Angel. "Does he know I am coming home?"

"All in the valley know and rejoice." Papá sent her a sly glance. "According to Emilio, chief among my wranglers although he is only twenty and five, 'The birds in the bushes will sing more sweetly and the flowers bloom more brightly because of Senorita Angelina's blessed presence.' "

Angel tittered. "If he handles horses as well as he speaks, this Emilio must be valuable to you. He has a way with words."

"Sí."

Angel looked at Conchita, who sat on the edge of her seat, listening with all her might. The desire for mischief rose, too strong to be denied. "Perhaps Emilio can teach Conchita to ride," she suggested in as innocent a tone as she could muster. "That is, when other duties do not claim him."

Conchita's eyes widened. Her mouth fell open, but no words came out.

If Papá noticed the girl's confusion, he ignored it. "That may be permissible. Emilio knows every caballo at the hacienda. Surely he can find one who is willing to carry you, Conchita."

A rich blush turned her olive skin rosy. "I — I —"

Angel took pity on her friend. "I will need to be taught as well," she reminded her father. "I venture to say none of the horses at La Casa del Sol has ever seen a side-saddle, let alone been forced to wear one."

"Well spoken." He threw his head back and laughed, but a moment later he turned serious. "You will both need to be skilled horsewomen. Even so, you are never to ride out alone. There are wild animals, bad-tempered cattle, and the danger of being thrown or left afoot. The great distances on the *rancho* make it easy to become lost, and much of the country looks the same."

He took a heavy silver watch from his pocket and consulted it. "It is no wonder that I begin to feel empty. Come. Let us go to the dining car."

"I am hungry, too." Angel followed him down the aisle with Conchita at her heels.

"You should be hungry," Conchita whis-

47

pered. "You didn't eat enough this morning to keep a gnat alive."

"I was too excited. Besides, you didn't eat any more than I did," Angel looked back over her shoulder and accused.

"I was too excited," Conchita mimicked.

Before Angel could turn around, the train swayed. Angel staggered. She reached for the edge of the aisle seat next to her in a desperate attempt to regain her balance . . . and missed. She fell against a young man's shoulder. If not for her victim's, "Whoa there, young lady," followed by two strong hands that gripped Angel's arms, she would have landed in her fellow passenger's lap!

Embarrassment rose like a river at flood tide. Angel wished she could crawl under a seat. Conchita's muffled titter didn't help.

Angel righted herself and stammered. *"Perdóneme."* When the young man looked blank, she added, "I mean, excuse me, please."

To her relief he smiled and reassured, "No harm done. Moving around in the cars can be worse than riding a bucking bronco."

His laugh relieved some of Angel's humiliation. Somewhat comforted but still flustered, she drew herself up to her full five foot five inches and looked straight ahead. Had Papá seen her mishap? Perhaps not.

His shoulders showed no sign of shaking with mirth.

The dining car was even more elegant than what Angel had seen from the station platform. But when they were seated, Conchita clutched her sleeve under cover of the fine tablecloth. Panic in her round face clearly showed the little maid felt she had strayed into a place where she ought not to be.

Angel laid a reassuring hand over Conchita's and sent her father a silent plea for help. To her relief, he responded by describing various items on the menu and suggesting food they might like. Conchita's hold gradually loosened. By the time the meal arrived, she had reverted to her normal self. But Angel realized it had been an ordeal for the younger girl. A wave of thankfulness for her father's handling of the situation washed through Angel. Her heart swelled with love and pride for the tall gracious man.

After dinner, the train chugged its way across land flatter than a tortilla, so different from San Francisco that Angel marveled. She and Conchita pressed their noses to the window glass and stared out, but fatigue and the monotony of the scenery took its toll. In spite of Angel's best efforts, she couldn't keep her eyes open. She fell asleep and didn't waken until a gentle hand shook her.

Her father's laughing voice followed the train whistle's mournful *wooo-ooo.* "Wake up, Angelina. We are in Fresno. Conchita is already awake."

The grinding screech of the train's great wheels slowed and stopped. Angel rubbed sleep from her eyes and sprang to her feet in alarm. "Why did you let me sleep?" she reproached.

Papá smiled. "I suspect you and Conchita got little sleep last night." He shrugged. "Besides, there was little to see except the flat land through which we have come. It will be much the same on our way to Madera, except since we are on the east side of the train, we may catch a glimpse of the Sierras."

Angel repressed the desire to shout with joy. "And then we go home."

"Sí." He stepped into the aisle. "Come. We must leave the train before other passengers board and we are carried away."

Conchita's eyes rounded with alarm, and her fingers bit into Angel's arm. "Would it do that, senor?"

"We will make sure it does not." He frowned. "Do you have veils?"

Angel nodded.

"Cover your faces. I do not wish you to be stared at." When they obeyed, he hurried them up the aisle, down the steps the porter had placed at edge of the passenger car, and onto the station platform.

Angel felt she had entered a new world. With her face hidden from curious stares, she was free to observe those who had gathered to meet the train. *Gringos.* Dark-skinned vaqueros such as Angel would find at La Casa del Sol. They wore checked or plaid shirts, colorful neckerchiefs, high-heeled boots, and wide hats or sombreros.

Her curious gaze moved on to blanketed Indians and a few dark-skinned women, some clad in black, others in red, white, and green, the colors of Mexico. A scattering of pigtailed Chinese and a horde of children with dogs completed Angel's survey. She would have liked to linger, but her father took her arm and led her into the station with Conchita close behind.

"We must wait a little while before boarding the train to Madera," he told them. "Would you like to take a walk?"

Angel nodded, but when they were on the train to Madera and her father went to the water cooler, she whispered to Conchita, "I will not tell Papá, but I am so anxious to

51

get to La Casa del Sol that I remember little about Fresno. Just the many kinds of people at the station." Conchita's ready giggle brought an answering smile to Angel's lips.

Papá returned and seated himself. "You may remove your veils now. Pray tell, what do you find so amusing?"

Angel fumbled with her veil, glad it provided a little time for the blush she felt burning her cheeks to recede. "We were speaking of those at the station." Laughter bubbled from her chest and spilled out. "Some of the men wore hats so wide it made them look like mushrooms!"

The screech of metal on metal when the train started drowned out the sounds of their merriment. The whistle's long *wooo-ooo* warned anyone foolish enough to step onto the tracks to get out of the way. Angel tingled from the toes of her well-shod feet to the top of her curly head. After what felt like a lifetime of banishment, she was really, truly on her way home.

FIVE

The first person Angel saw when she stepped down from the train in Madera and onto the wooden platform in front of Moore's General Store and Post Office was her old proprietor friend. Except for being more portly and balder than ever, he looked very much the way she remembered. He beamed at her.

"Well, well, 'pears to me you've grown into a mighty fine young lady," Evan said.

"Gracias." Angel blinked back tears at the warm greeting. "Has the town grown? I only remember your store and a hotel, where we went to eat sometimes."

"Captain Russell Perry Mace's Yosemite Hotel. Still the finest in town." Evan sighed. "We miss the captain now that he's gone. I can still see him in that tall hat he always wore." He peered at Conchita. "And who is this?" He guffawed. "Senor Montoya, you'll have to chase the boys off with a stick once

53

they get wind there are two pretty girls at the House of the Sun."

"I think not." The words fell like ice pellets, followed by the drum of horses' hooves and the arrival of a carriage drawn by two high-stepping bays. "Come, Angelina, Conchita. Our driver is here."

Angel stiffened at the chill in her father's voice.

"No offense," a red-faced Evan Moore mumbled.

"None taken." But Papá's tone of voice belied the words. He hurried the girls into the carriage and sat stiff as a poker. *Why did he act like that?* Angel wondered. *Young senors will surely call.* The thought make her tingle. She'd never had a suitor. Tía Guadalupe had complained more than once about Papá's edict against allowing such a thing.

Angel's heart thumped. Would her father continue to forbid suitors? What of Conchita? Her sweetness and natural beauty would without doubt attract those seeking a good wife. She had been attractive in her servant's dress. Garbed now in clothing Angel had taken from her own wardrobe and insisted she wear, Conchita was lovely. Oh dear, so many new things to consider!

Angel stared at the western sky. It flamed like the blaze that had consumed a home

54

not far from the Garcias in San Francisco: red, purple, and orange against a vivid blue. It reminded Angel of evenings when the sun painted the sky over the ocean before slowly sinking in the distance. "How long will it take to get home, Papá?"

The ice in his voice had melted. "Not long. See how rapidly the horses go? Juan is a good driver." He patted Angel's hand.

Satisfied, she leaned back against his shoulder and strained her eyes for her first glimpse of La Casa del Sol. At last her searching gaze was rewarded. The carriage topped a slight rise, and the House of the Sun appeared before them.

Long and low, the hacienda's pale ivory stucco walls shone in the light of the dying sun as if painted with gold. Angel fancied it held out flower-laden arms to welcome them. She had seen bougainvillea in San Francisco but not like this. Great clusters of red and purple flowers cascaded from the red-tiled roof to the ground. Gigantic oaks stood on guard inside the ornate iron fence, which matched grilles around the windows.

For a heartbeat Angel was a child again: a child who refused to look back at the home she loved. She had known that if she turned for a final glimpse she could never leave. Now she bit back a sob and raised her chin.

Dios had brought her back to where she belonged. She would let no sad memories spoil her homecoming.

"Have you seen her?"

Tim Sterling scowled at his sister, Ellie, who smiled at him from beside the Diamond S corral. A horse and buggy stood nearby. He dropped Blue's reins and limped toward her. "The only thing I've seen is two dusty miles of walking. Blue picked up a stone. It's not too bad, but I had to hoof it home." Tim snorted like a wheezing horse. "Wouldn't you know, there wasn't anyone around for a million miles."

Sympathy filled Ellie's blue eyes. "No wonder you're out of sorts."

Tim snorted. "Out of sorts? Ha! Ever tried leading a lame horse and walking in riding boots? My feet feel like two slabs of raw beef." He led Blue to a water trough and let him drink. "Be back in a minute." Waves of weariness washed over him as he took Blue to the barn and turned him over to a wrangler with orders to care for the horse's injured foot.

He returned to find Ellie had moved from the corral to the wide veranda of the hacienda-style ranch house, home to Tim for the past ten years. He hobbled up the

56

walk and parked on the top step. Several hard jerks freed his feet from their dusty boots. Tim removed his socks, flexed his cramped toes, and examined his aching feet.

"Any blisters?"

"Naw. Just redder than the morning sky before a gully washer." He looked around the empty porch. "So where's everyone?" He rolled his eyes. "Don't tell me. With Timmy, right?"

Ellie's eyes twinkled. "You guessed it. I have to play second fiddle when my son is around. Sarah kidnapped him when I first got here."

A burst of laughter floated through the open doorway, followed by a high-pitched voice demanding, "Coo-kie, S'lita."

"So that's where he is, the little rascal." Ellie stood. "I'd better go rescue him before Matt's beloved housekeeper spoils him rotten."

Tim shook his head. "She won't. She'll love him, feed him cookies, and doctor his knees and elbows when he scrapes them, just like she did for us. But she won't spoil him." He stood and followed Ellie to the large kitchen. Sarah and Solita sat at the large table with Timmy on the diminutive housekeeper's lap. Her smiling face looked little different to Tim than when he and Ellie had first come to the Diamond S.

"Unca Tim!" Timmy slid to the floor and raced across the tile floor. His crumb-covered hands completed the ruination of Tim's sweat-stained britches when he stepped on his uncle's feet and grabbed his legs.

Tim grimaced and lifted the child back onto the floor. "Whoa there, buckaroo."

"Up horsey?" Timmy wanted to know.

"Not today. Blue hurt his foot."

Timmy's lower lip stuck out, but he brightened when Solita patted her lap and said, "Come here, *niñito.*" She wrinkled her nose. "Senor Tim smells like his horse. He needs to find a bath instead of dawdling in my clean kitchen."

Tim chuckled in spite of his pain. "I never could get by with anything, could I, Solita? May I have a cookie?"

Her eyes twinkled, and she pointed to the door. "When you return."

Tim gave an exaggerated sigh. "Sí, Little Sun. Just don't let Timmy eat all the cookies before I get back." He departed in a wave of laughter that warmed his heart. Solita had ruled the Diamond S with a rod of love ever since Matt Sterling was a boy, bringing sunshine to generations of children. *God, please keep her strong and*

58

healthy so she can someday be here for mine.

The unbidden thought stopped Tim in his tracks. His mouth fell open. A strange prayer for a fancy-free cowboy with fewer prospects for a wife and children than for finding nuggets in a played-out gold mine.

Tim rid himself of trail grime and doused himself until he reeked with what he privately called "stinkum" filched from the bunkhouse. He considered the cheap hair tonic an abomination, but it was the perfect payback for Solita's remark.

After donning a clean shirt, vest, and pants, he sashayed back to the house and into the kitchen. Ellie leaped up from her chair and made a terrible face. "Timothy Sterling, what have you done to yourself?" She snatched a handkerchief from the sleeve of her gown and held it over her nose.

Tim rounded his eyes and put on his most innocent, aggrieved tone. "Solita said I smelled like a horse."

"You smell worse now," Sarah put in, but Tim suspected she wanted to laugh.

"So where are my cookies, Solita?" he inquired.

She looked toward heaven in the way Tim knew meant a prayer for patience; then she grabbed a handful of cookies and thrust them at him. "Go. The veranda is the place

59

for you."

Tim took the cookies but fired a parting shot. "I'll go, since no one here seems to appreciate me. I'll bet Blue still loves me." Tim snatched an apple from the bowl on the table and started out. Ellie followed him. Once seated in rocking chairs on the porch Tim stuffed cookies in his mouth and remembered something. "Hey, when I got here you asked if I'd seen her. Who is 'her'?"

"Angelina Carmencita Olivera Montoya."

Tim blinked. "What a name. Can you imagine hanging it on anyone?"

Ellie tittered. "I probably would if I were Don Fernando."

"The owner of La Casa del Sol?"

"The same."

"So, what does Don Fernando have to do with Angelina what's-her-name?"

His sister's eyes glistened. "She's his eighteen-year-old daughter, who has been living in San Francisco since she was six."

"Why?" Not that he cared. Some girl who had been in San Francisco for two years before he and Ellie came to the valley was nothing in his life.

"The story is that when the girl's mother died, her father was so grief stricken he allowed an aunt and uncle to take her to San Francisco until she turned eighteen. Now

60

she's come home. According to rumors, her father is already searching for a husband for Angelina."

Tim snorted and bit into his apple. "Is she so ugly she can't find one of her own?"

"Not if she has kept her looks. Sarah said Angelina was a black-eyed beauty as a child. There will be no lack of applicants for her hand. Besides, she will eventually inherit La Casa del Sol. Her husband will be *patrón* of the huge estate after the death of Don Fernando."

"You are getting to be a terrible gossip," Tim accused.

Ellie smirked. "I am not. A minister's wife needs to be *informed* about what is happening." She gathered her skirts and rose.

Tim sat up straight. It would never do to let Ellie leave, knowing she had gotten the best of him. "Hey, maybe I should apply for the job of patrón."

"You!" Ellie gaped and dropped back into her chair. "You'd have less chance of marrying Angel Montoya than of the sun rising in the west. She's not only the apple of her father's eye; she's the whole orchard."

"According to gossip?" Tim jeered. "Besides, what's wrong with me?" He swelled his chest and hooked his thumbs in his vest. "I consider myself a fine figger of a man."

"It wouldn't matter if you were the best-looking rider in California," Ellie told him. "Don Fernando will arrange the marriage of his daughter to a wealthy hacendado who can continue the Castilian bloodline." She crossed her arms and glared at him. "If you have any wild ideas about Angel Montoya, get rid of them right now."

Tim leaned his chair back until it turned over. He fell to the veranda floor and laughed until tears came. "Got your goat, didn't I?" he chortled.

"I mean what I say," Ellie snapped. "Angel Montoya is not for the likes of you. I'm getting Timmy and leaving before you take further leave of your senses." She whirled into the house and banged the door behind her.

Tim scrambled to his feet. "Aw, Ellie, I'm only teasing." But when she came out with Timmy in tow and marched past him on her way to the buggy, Tim couldn't help giving a final dig. "So, Senorita Montoya is called Angel. Hmmm. She doesn't sound like anyone I'd be interested in, even if I was looking for a girl." He hastily added, "Which I'm not."

Ellie smirked, good humor obviously restored. "Don't tempt fate, little brother. One of these days . . ." She raised her shoulders in an expressive gesture, herded Timmy into the buggy, and followed him. A taunting smile and a quick flick of the reins started the buggy toward town, leaving Tim to stare after it. He hadn't gotten the last word after all.

Six

The day after Angel reached La Casa del Sol, her father introduced her and Conchita to Emilio Sanchez and ordered him to make skilled horsewomen of them.

The head wrangler's black eyes shone. His teeth flashed white against his smooth, dark skin. "Sí, senor." He struck his chest in a dramatic gesture. "I, Emilio Sanchez, will do so with great haste."

Angel wanted to laugh but restrained herself. So might a knight of old pledge allegiance to his king. Suspecting that Conchita might erupt in a giggle, Angel shot her a warning glance. Emilio appeared in dead earnest. It would be cruel to spoil his declared devotion.

Angel found herself an unwilling witness to a remarkable conversation a few days later. Needing to ask her father about a household matter, she tapped on the open door of his office. When she received no answer, she stepped inside and crossed to the open window overlooking the courtyard around which the house was built. She breathed in the perfume from masses of brightly blooming flowers; then her gaze traveled to the fountain. Its waters created rainbows in the sunlight and fell into a pool, where birds splashed and split the still air with their songs. "If I live to be an old woman I will never tire of our courtyard," she vowed. "Can any place be more peaceful?"

A voice from the hall outside the office broke into Angel's enjoyment. "Por favor, senor. May I speak with you?"

"What is it, Emilio?" Papá sounded impatient.

Angel's heart fluttered. Oh, dear. Was Emilio dissatisfied with how the riding lessons were going? What should she do? Call out and make her presence known? She gathered her full yellow skirt around her and took a step toward the door. But she froze when Emilio said, "I wish to have your permission to pay my addresses to the senorita."

"You what?" Papá's roar nearly deafened Angel. "How dare you ask such a thing? My daughter is not to be pursued by such as you. She will marry a man of my choosing.

65

Now leave the hacienda before I have you horsewhipped!"

Angel clapped her hand over her mouth to keep from crying out. Surely Papá did not mean what he said. She wanted to rush across the room and plead with him not to hurt Emilio, but her feet felt nailed to the floor.

A loud gasp followed before the would-be suitor's voice rose in what sounded like horror. "Senor! I, Emilio Sanchez, swear by all the saints. It is not the blessed Angelina's favor this poor *peón* wishes to seek. It is the hand of the beautiful Conchita. From the very moment I saw her, my heart beat like thunder."

Angel heard a loud sigh, then a mournful, "If she does not love me, surely I die."

"Enough of your foolishness, Emilio," her father snapped. "Get back to your duties. I will think about this and give you my answer later."

"Sí, senor." The sound of boot heels on the tiled floor signified both men had gone.

Angel sagged against the window frame. Relief swept through her. It had been all she could do to stifle the laughter that would have betrayed her presence.

"I suppose I should be sorry for eavesdropping even though it wasn't my fault," she whispered. "I'm not. I can hardly wait to tell Conchita that the handsome Emilio thinks she is beautiful and says he will surely die if she does not love him." A thrill went through her. One look had made Emilio brave as a mountain lion, brave enough to present himself to Don Fernando. "If Conchita is willing, will Papá allow Emilio to carry on a courtship?"

Angel's heart skipped a beat. Was there a way for her to help? Perhaps if she confessed she had overheard the conversation? No! Proud as she knew her father to be, he would not want his daughter to know he had first thought Emilio aspired to her hand!

Angel stifled a giggle. She tiptoed across the room into the hall and checked both ways. It stretched long and empty. Angel gathered her full skirt and rustling petticoats around her and raced up the winding staircase to the second story. Breathless from running, she burst into the spacious bedroom that had been kept the way she left it twelve years before.

Its warmth enveloped her. Her rooms at the Garcias' had been furnished with heirloom furniture, exquisite but dark. Here all was light. Walls the color of sunflowers glowed. A well-padded window seat flanked casement windows that opened wide and overlooked the courtyard. A gold, red, and orange tapestry highlighted with a touch of green covered the bed. Drapes of the same green hung at the windows and covered two chairs. White tiles gleamed from the open door of Angel's private bathroom. But the focal point of the bedroom was a portrait of Angel's mother that smiled down from above the capacious fireplace.

Angel tapped on the door that connected her room with Conchita's. Papá had at first demurred at having the younger girl in the main house but agreed on the condition Conchita be considered Angel's personal maid.

"I know she is your amiga, but there must be no cause for jealousy among the other servants," he had said.

Now Angel chuckled. "There will be plenty of jealousy if Emilio is given permission to pay his addresses to Conchita! No one with two eyes in her head could miss how admired he is — especially by the unmarried girls." She tapped again. "I wonder where Conchita is."

"Here senorita." Conchita's face shone above a snowy-white blouse and full, scarlet skirt.

Angel turned. Her friend stood in the doorway to the hall, arms piled high with fluffy towels. No matter how many times Angel told her to leave such duties to those who did general housework, Conchita persisted in waiting on her mistress. Now she crossed to the bathroom, loaded the towel racks with her booty, then smiled. "Did you need me?"

Angel grabbed her by the waist and whirled her into a wild dance that landed them on the bed, disheveled and laughing. "What do you think of Emilio?"

Conchita blinked. "He is a good teacher. Already, the little brown horse he gives me to ride is willing."

Angel grunted. "I don't mean as a riding teacher. How would you feel about Emilio as a suitor?"

Disbelief filled Conchita's eyes, and her mouth fell open. "A suitor! Why do you ask such a thing? Sooner will the sky fall on our heads."

Angel lowered her voice to a mysterious pitch. "Wrong. This very afternoon I heard Emilio ask Papá's permission to seek your favor."

"Impossible."

"Have I ever told you a falsehood?"

Conchita clenched her hands. "Perhaps you misunderstood."

Excitement rushed through Angel's veins

until she could barely contain her glee. "I heard him with my very own ears. Emilio said, 'This poor peón wishes to seek the hand of the beautiful Conchita. From the very moment I saw her, my heart beat like thunder. If she does not love me, surely I die.' "

Conchita fell back against a ruffled pillow. She opened her mouth, but no words came out. Tears left glistening streaks down her smooth brown cheeks.

Angel's high spirits dropped to her toes. Never in a million years had she suspected Conchita would cry. "I — I thought you would be happy," she faltered.

The smile that broke over her friend's face rivaled a rainbow after rain. "I cannot believe it is true. When we have the riding lesson, my heart thumps until I am afraid Senor Sanchez will hear and think I am the *chica tonta.*"

"You are not a stupid girl. You are in love."

"Sí," Conchita whispered. "Will your Papá give his permission?"

Angel patted her hand. "We will pray that it will be so."

After Conchita had gone, Angel crossed to the window seat and stared down into the courtyard. An emotion she had never before felt swelled within her: envy — and the wish someone cared for her as Emilio and Conchita already cared for each other.

Memory of her father's words to Emilio interrupted the thought before Angel could fully explore it: *"My daughter is not to be pursued by such as you. She will marry a man of my choosing."*

"How could I have been so excited about Emilio's declaration that I wasn't paying attention to anything else?" she wondered. A chill ran up her spine. She would never forget her father's icy response to Evan Moore's observation about the young men pursuing her and Conchita: *"I think not."*

Tía Guadalupe's complaints about her niece not being allowed to have male callers flashed across Angel's mind. What did Papá have in mind for her? What if she met someone and fell in love as Emilio and Conchita had done? Angel shivered and thrust the question aside. She could trust her father to do what was best.

Or could she?

For the next few weeks, Angel was so busy and happy that fear of the future faded. Her father had presented her with a belated birthday gift: a magnificent horse named *La Mujer Blanca* — White Woman. Angel spent every spare moment with her.

Papá had also given Emilio permission to win Conchita's heart. "Not that it will take much," he told Angel. "She has the same look in her eyes when she looks at Emilio that my Carmencita wore when we first met. It never changed." He strode away before Angel could reply, but not before she saw the pain in his eyes.

Would such a great love come to her? A love even death could not kill? "I want no other kind," Angel whispered. But as the days slipped by and she watched the love grow between Emilio and Conchita, the chambers of her heart felt empty.

One afternoon just before La Casa del Sol settled down for its daily siesta, a servant rapped on Angel's door. "Senor Montoya wishes la senorita to come to his office."

What can Papá want? Angel questioned as she hurried down the stairs. It wasn't like him to interrupt the time of rest he insisted on during the worst heat of the day. She found him seated behind his massive desk.

"A letter from Tía Guadalupe."

Angel dropped into a leather chair. "You look happy. It must contain good news."

"Very." He held out a newspaper clipping. "From the *San Francisco Chronicle.*"

Why should anything in a city newspaper please her father so? Angel wondered, but she obediently took the clipping and read the article:

MEXICAN VISITOR TALK OF THE TOWN

San Francisco is hailing with delight the arrival of Ramon Chavez. The Mexican hacendado comes to our fair city armed with impeccable credentials. Reputed to have vast holdings in his own country, Chavez also has several commendations, including those from the government for meritorious service in the Mexican Army. These, coupled with the fact he is an eligible bachelor, have given him entrée into San Francisco's best circles. Happy hunting, ladies.

The picture below the article showed a middle-aged man whose eyes bored into Angel's. Eyebrows thick and dark as his moustache crawled across his forehead like an overgrown caterpillar. No trace of a smile softened the swarthy, rock-hard face.

The picture made Angel shudder without knowing why, but before she could speak, her father said, "You need to hear Tía's letter." He spread out the pages. "She sends love and greetings, and then she says:

"I have wonderful news. The enclosed clipping is part of it. Ramon Chavez is here in the city on business. Miguel and I are fortunate to be among those to whom he brought letters of introduction. He is an answer to our prayers for Angelina. What could be better than for you to arrange a marriage with a man of such great wealth? He is older than Angelina, but she will never lack for anything.

"Senor Chavez has shown us photographs of his hacienda. It is spectacular.

"We told him about Angelina and showed him her picture. He wants to come to Madera to meet her. Or would you prefer to come here? We feel blessed that Dios has provided a suitable match for our dear niece. . . ."

Angel sprang to her feet. Horror at the very thought of marriage with a man like the one in the picture gripped her throat with icy fingers. "There will be no match," she cried. "He is old enough to be my father. Almost old enough to be my grandfather!"

Shock replaced the pleased look on Papá's face. He shoved his chair back from the desk so hard it crashed to the floor. "Be still. It is not your place to make such a decision. I am your father, and I will do what I know is best for you. There is nothing wrong with marrying an older man. This Ramon Chavez sounds most suitable. He can carry on the pure Castilian bloodline that we trace back for hundreds of years."

Angel cowered but only for a heartbeat. "I would rather die than belong to that man!" She ran from the room as if pursued by a thousand devils, all of them wearing Ramon Chavez's face.

SEVEN

Angel tottered into her room, locked the door, and threw herself on her bed. Her face burned, and she gulped back great sobs. Would Papá really force her to wed a man against her will? A man she instinctively disliked and feared?

Sí, a little voice inside her said. *If Senor Chavez is the wealthy hacendado he is reported to be, there will be no escape.*

Angel beat her fist against a pillow. "What if he is not?"

Why do you think such a thing? the voice taunted. *You know how particular the Garcias are. They would not recommend a suitor unless he is all he claims to be.*

Despair made Angel's stomach churn. She sprang to her feet and stared at the golden walls that felt as if they were closing in on her until she would be crushed. Her mind raced.

"I have to get away and think before I see

Papá again," she whispered. Determination filled her. "There will be no better time than now, during the siesta."

Angel started toward Conchita's door then shook her head. It was best not to involve her friend. Instead, she quickly removed her afternoon dress and donned her riding habit. Her need to escape the room that now felt like a jail supported her plan to ride out alone, even though it was strictly forbidden.

With a quick prayer that she would not be discovered, Angel slipped out of her door and tiptoed down the hall to a back stairway. Step by cautious step, she descended and stole through the courtyard. Only the lazy hum of bees disturbed the silence. Even the birds must be taking a siesta. "I hope I can ride Blanca without a saddle," Angel muttered as she sneaked to the tack room and snatched a bridle. "I don't dare bring her up here, and a saddle's too heavy to carry out to the pasture."

It felt like hours before she reached the pasture, where a dozen horses dozed in the lazy afternoon. Not a vaquero was in sight. A small miracle. Now to whistle for Blanca. She shaded her eyes with her hand and stared out over the pasture. Her joy over having been undetected so far died a-borning. White Woman was nowhere to be seen.

"There are plenty of other horses," Angel told herself. "Call one and go!" She whistled loud enough for the horses to hear but too low for the sound to carry to the house. A few horses trotted to the fence. Angel hesitated. The only one small enough for her to straddle was a pinto pony that Emilio had not yet allowed her to ride.

"The *caballito,* some days he is the angel. On other days I fear he has been eating loco weed." Emilio had spread his hands wide and rolled his eyes.

Angel's need to get away sent caution flying. With a prayer that this was one of the animal's angelic days, she patted his soft nose. "I don't have a choice. Will you please stand still?"

The pinto shied away, but after several tries Angel managed to stop his dancing enough to bridle him and mount. Lacking the security of a saddle, she held the reins tightly, clamped her legs to the pony's sides, and nudged him forward with her knees.

Things went well for a time. The pinto appeared content to amble at a pace in tune with the lazy day. Angel began to adjust to riding bareback. Determined to get as far as possible from the house, she paid little attention to the way they were headed.

A delicious sense of freedom settled over her like a soft mantilla. "This is one of the few times I can remember being on my own," Angel mused.

The pony flicked one ear and headed for a stand of oak trees.

She made a face. "As if you care. You are able to run free in the pasture. If Papá forces me to marry Senor Chavez, I shall be a caged bird."

When they reached the shaded area, a *whirr* of wings blended with a low, chattering sound. A quail rose from its ground nest directly in front of them. The pinto snorted, reared, and came down stiff-legged.

Angel's teeth chattered from the jolt. She held on for dear life but felt herself slipping. Seconds later the horse pitched again. Angel flew into the air. She heard the sound of galloping hooves but had no time to roll. She crashed to the ground and landed on her left shoulder. Pain shot down her arm, so intense she cried out. Then merciful blackness claimed her.

Tim Sterling swung his well-worn saddle over Blue's back and sang out, *"Did you ever hear tell of Sweet Betsy from Pike,/Who crossed the wide mountains with her lover*

79

Ike,/Two yoke of cattle, a large yeller dog,/A tall Shanghai rooster, and a one-spotted hog./ Singing too-ra-li-oo-ra-li-oo-ra-li-ay. Singing —"

A laughing voice interrupted. "You're in a mighty good mood today." Matt Sterling grinned at Tim from his perch on the top rail of the Diamond S corral.

Tim finished saddling Blue. "A feller's just gotta sing on a day like this." He added a "yodel-lay-ee-oh-de-lay-ee-oh-delay-ee" in a high falsetto, but its effect was spoiled when his voice cracked on a high note.

Blue danced away, and Matt put both hands over his ears. "I gotta tell you, Tim. You'll never outsing that sister of yours."

Tim cocked one eyebrow. "So? One Sierra Songbird in the family's enough."

Matt laughed then turned serious. "Where are you riding today?"

A warning bell rang in Tim's brain. "Town, I hope. I'm hankerin' to hear some of Ellie's warbling."

"No chance. I need you to check out the property line between us and the Montoyas. There's a stretch of fence that may need mending."

There went hopes of a trip to town. "Aw, Matt, you know I hate mending fences worse than poison."

"Sorry. It has to be done, and the rest of the hands are long gone." A teasing look came into his eyes. "Look at it this way. You may catch a glimpse of the 'oh so beautiful' senorita." Matt clasped his hands and gazed up with a sappy expression.

Tim made a disgusted sound. "You look like a moonstruck calf." He went to the barn for the tools he would need for the hated job and stowed them in his saddlebags.

Matt returned to his subject like a deer to a salt lick. "From what I hear, Angelina Carmencita Olivera Montoya is worth it." The name fairly rolled off his tongue.

Tim grimaced. "Still can't see why anyone would saddle an innocent kid with that name."

Matt shrugged. "Logical. Her mother was Carmencita Olivera. If Angel looks like her, she'll be quite a picture on that white horse Don Fernando gave her. La Mujer Blanca is reported to be the most beautiful mare at La Casa del Sol." Matt chuckled.

Tim smirked and pitched his voice to that of a simpering female. "Oh, dear me, how ever do I make this horse go?"

Matt laughed until he swayed and had to grab the fence rail to keep from tumbling off. "You are way behind times, Timothy. According to Emilio Sanchez, who is teaching Angel and her friend Conchita to ride, 'The blessed senorita rides astride and goes like the wind.' "

Suspicion flared into a frown. "How come you know so much about her?"

"I have ways," Matt derided. "Besides, I have a wife and sister who keep me informed. And hands who are so envious of Emilio's being able to spend time with two beautiful young ladies they are gnashing their teeth. You have to admire Sanchez. He asked and received Don Fernando's permission to court Conchita before the other boys could do more than gape at her!"

Matt bent a meaningful glance at Tim, who guessed what was coming. "That's the way to win a girl's hand. Take her by storm."

Tim swung to the saddle. "Thank you for the lesson in how to impress young ladies, Mr. Know-it-all." Sarcasm underscored every word. "Now if you don't mind, I'll get to work." He sent Blue into a gallop. But he couldn't outrun Matt's stentorian taunt:

"Watch out for beautiful dark-eyed senoritas riding snow-white horses!"

"Buffalo chips," Tim grumbled. "Beautiful, dark-eyed senoritas take siestas this time of day. They aren't out riding snow-white horses, or any other color horse, for that matter." He pushed back his Stetson and mopped his forehead. "Whew. It's too hot for anything but rattlesnakes. No good for poor, miserable cowboys who hate mending fences."

The tantalizing thought of a pitcher of ice-cold lemonade and a hammock under a spreading oak tree turned the corners of Tim's mouth down. He patted Blue's neck. "Well, the sooner we get done checking out the fence, the quicker we can mosey on home."

Tim's attention turned back to his conversation with Matt. In spite of himself, he couldn't help feeling curious about Angel Montoya. "What kind of girl is she anyway?" he asked Blue. "Probably a sissy girl who giggles and blushes every time a man looks at her. Ugh." The next moment, Tim reluctantly shook his head. "Gotta admit, Old Man. If the senorita rides astride and goes like the wind, she's no sissy. Hmmm. Wonder if she lives up to her name?" He let out a whoop of disbelief. "She sounds too good to be true. And when things sound that way, they usually aren't."

Blue whinnied and tossed his head but kept a steady pace. Busy with his thoughts, Tim reached the fence that separated the vast Montoya holdings from the Diamond S range. Another half-hour's ride brought him to a break in the fence. Tim reset two posts and tightened the wire. "Glad that's done." He put his tools back in his saddle-bags and started to mount. The sound of pounding hooves stopped him.

"What the — ?" Tim stared. A wild-eyed pinto pony charged past him on the other side of the fence as if in fear of his life. Tim's mouth fell open. No saddle, just a bridle, and terror in every quivering muscle. Tim looked both ways. The flat land stretched calm and peaceful in the late afternoon sunlight, as far as he could see. Nothing appeared responsible for stampeding the pinto into a dead run. Yet the inborn sense of something amiss developed by long years on the range kept Tim from shrugging the incident off and heading for home.

"What's that pony doing out here by himself?" he wondered aloud. "There's no sign of a herd anywhere, but who would be riding bareback?" Tim heaved a deep sigh. "Well, standing here jawing about it won't give any answers. We've gotta go see."

He loosened the wire he had just tightened around the fence posts and folded it back to allow enough space for Blue to step through onto Montoya property. Once there, Tim put the wire back. "All that work for nothing," he complained. "Can't be helped, though. If someone got thrown, he could be hurt, and there's not much chance of anyone finding him out here."

Tim vaulted into the saddle and headed Blue in the direction the pinto had come. The terrified pony's hooves had flattened the parched grass enough to leave a trail.

Twenty minutes later, Tim's keen gaze caught sight of something lying in a heap under a large oak tree a short distance away. His heart thundered. He urged Blue into a run. In a flash they reached the shaded spot. A girl lay motionless on the ground. In contrast to the tumbled black hair peeping from under a sombrero, her face was whiter than the lacy blouse beneath a black vest that matched her riding skirt.

Matt's words rang in Tim's ears. *"Watch out for beautiful dark-eyed senoritas riding snow-white horses!"*

Tim brushed away the thought. There was no snow-white horse. Just a crumpled girl in disheveled clothing. He sprang from the saddle and breathed a prayer: *Please God, don't let her be dead.*

EIGHT

Please God, don't let her be dead, Tim silently repeated. His brain spun. Why had the girl who lay at his feet been riding bareback and alone? How long had she been unconscious? Tim brushed the questions aside. Time enough for that later. He knelt beside the girl, checked her pulse, and let out a sigh of relief. Strong and steady. Tim snatched his canteen from the saddle horn. He tore off his neckerchief, soaked it with water, and gently bathed the girl's face.

The dark lashes that made half moons against her pale cheeks fluttered. A moment later, her eyes opened, great dark gulfs whose beauty brought back Seth's teasing: *"I can see it all now. Tim's gonna be one of those galoots who falls in love at first sight."*

Hard on its heels came his own reply: *"When the San Joaquin River runs dry. Love at first sight is a myth or for the weak minded."*

Tim's heart lurched. Maybe so, but why

did those dazed eyes make him feel he'd just been hit by a battering ram?

"Who are you? Where am I?" The girl shook her head as if trying to clear it.

Tim laid one hand on her shoulder. "Don't try to move. I'm Timothy Sterling, better known as Tim. An ornery pinto threw you then hightailed it for home. Can you move your arms and legs?"

She uncurled from her crumpled position and straightened her legs, then her right arm. When she flexed her left arm, she moaned and clutched her shoulder. She didn't cry, but her expression showed what the movement cost. "I don't think it's broken," she said through gritted teeth. "But it hurts."

"Probably sprained," Tim told her. "We've got to get you home, but first, drink this." He held his canteen to her lips and was rewarded by a bit of color returning to her face after she drank.

Tim burned to know why she had been riding a cantankerous pony without a saddle so far from home, but something in her demeanor stopped him. Unless he was sadly mistaken, Don Fernando's daughter — and that's who she must be — wouldn't take kindly to being questioned, even by her rescuer. Instead he asked, "Did you hit your head when you fell?"

"No. It was the pain in my shoulder and arm that caused me to faint. I will be all right, Senor Sterling. Truly."

"My friends call me Tim," he told her. "And you are Senorita Angelina Carmencita Olivera Montoya?"

"Sí. My friends call me Angel."

"Are you an angel?" It slipped out before Tim could bite his tongue.

A shadow crept into her eyes, and she shook her head. "N–not always."

Again Tim wanted to question her. He could not. It would be impertinent to try and discover what she meant by her cryptic reply. And what had caused the sadness in her face? "We need to get going. Does anyone know where you are?"

"No."

The word hung flat and unexplained in the afternoon air.

Tim bound Angel's injured arm with his neckerchief to help immobilize it, then carried her to Blue. Once in the saddle with her in his arms, Tim headed toward La Casa del Sol with mixed emotions. He could just imagine what his family would say when they learned he had rescued the "blessed senorita."

Admiration welled up inside Tim. His

brief acquaintance with Angel Montoya showed he'd been right about one thing: this was no sissy girl. She flinched now and then from the motion of the horse but didn't complain even though he knew her arm and shoulder must be hurting.

He hoped she couldn't hear the hard thud of his traitorous heart where she lay across his chest. Every beat taunted. *You can never again say there's no such thing as love at first sight. You're hooked tighter than Matt and Sarah, who fell in love with each other's pictures. And Josh and Ellie, when she tripped and fell down at the fiesta. What made you think you could escape?*

Angel squirmed, trying to get her aching arm and shoulder into a more comfortable position. Perhaps if she concentrated on what had transpired since she left the House of the Sun, she could get her mind off the pain. Things seemed fuzzy until she sailed off the pinto's back and landed in the shade of the oak tree. How long had she lain unconscious before Senor Sterling had found her? What if he hadn't? She suppressed a shudder. Sooner or later Papá would have discovered she was missing, but no one would have dreamed she'd taken off on an unsaddled horse — a horse about which she had been warned!

Regret filled her. Why had she thought she could outrun her problems? All she had done was show she could not be trusted. Angel swallowed hard. She wished she had drunk more deeply from the canteen, even though the water was brackish. She relived the moment when she awakened to find the tall cowboy kneeling at her side. Memory of the concern in his brown eyes and the gentle way he had cared for her brought a rush of gratitude.

Angel allowed her head to rest more firmly against Tim's chest. The steady beat of his heart lulled her and brought a feeling that nothing could harm her when she was with him. Yet even that thought could not defeat the lassitude stealing over her. Try as she would, Angel could not keep her eyes open.

She awoke to hear Tim say, "Whoa, Blue. We're here," followed by a multitude of voices chattering in Spanish and English. It sounded like the entire staff of La Casa del Sol was present. Conchita stood in their midst, one hand over her mouth. Her eyes looked enormous — and fearful.

Papá's deep tones rose above the babble. "I'll take her. Is she hurt?"

Angel felt herself transferred to her father's strong arms.

"Her left arm and shoulder appear to be sprained," Tim replied.

"Where did you find her?" Papá demanded.

"I was fixing the fence on our property line. An unsaddled pinto flew past on your side of the fence. When Blue and I investigated, we found your daughter."

"A pinto? Unsaddled? Emilio!" her father roared. "What is the meaning of this?"

Angel roused herself enough to come to the head wrangler's defense. "It is not Emilio's fault, Papá. I made sure no one saw me when I slipped away during siesta. Even Conchita didn't know I was going."

There. It was out. Now Tim would know she was not as angelic as her name. Ignoring her aching arm and shoulder, she freed herself from her father's arms and stood on her feet. She glanced at her rescuer and had the sneaking suspicion he wanted to laugh. "Senor Sterling found me after the pony threw me," she said in a low voice. "He kindly brought me home."

The rigidity of her father's jaw did not change. "Gracias a Dios," he muttered, then held out a hand and gripped Tim's.

"Glad to be of service." Tim released the older man's hand and touched his Stetson. "I'll ride over soon and see that you're no

91

worse for your fall, senorita."

Angel saw her father scowl, but gratefulness gave her the courage to wordlessly nod. She wanted to know Timothy better. To discover why the look of admiration in his face called to something within her, a feeling she had never before experienced.

Angel watched the dark-haired young cowboy ride out of sight, remembering how protected she had felt in his arms. Then she turned to face the results of her escapade — consequences promised by the warning flash in her father's eyes.

The sun disappeared long before Tim and Blue reached the Diamond S. A soft purple haze formed, soon replaced by a multitude of stars and a lopsided moon that bathed the land in a silver glow. Its radiance was surpassed only by the glow in Tim's veins. The distant cry of a coyote shattered the stillness of the night. It made Tim shiver. Angel could still be out there alone and frightened if he hadn't come along.

"Thanks, God." He chuckled. "She may be Senorita Angelina Carmencita Olivera Montoya, but she's Angel to me." Every moment of their time together played back in his mind. Tim slouched in the saddle and confided to Blue, "The proud senor didn't seem thrilled at the idea of my visiting the hacienda. I'll go, though. He didn't say I couldn't. I'll get myself duded up in my best Sunday-go-to-meeting clothes and pay me a call just as soon as I can get away from Matt's eagle eye. I'm not gonna tell him or anyone at the Diamond S that I rescued Angel. They'd never let me hear the last of it!"

He let out a mighty yawn. "Get along, horse. I'm ready to hit the hay." Blue responded by quickening his pace.

Long after Tim's head rested on his feather pillow, he stared out his bedroom window and watched the stars.

Words from a favorite psalm came to mind: *"When I consider thy heavens, the work of thy fingers, the moon and the stars, which thou hast ordained; What is man, that thou art mindful of him? and the son of man, that thou visitest him? For thou hast made him a little lower than the angels, and hast crowned him with glory and honour."*

Tim smothered a laugh in his pillow. "Well, God, this man is a lot lower than one Angel Montoya, and so far I haven't earned much glory or honor. But I'll be a petrified jackrabbit if she didn't look happy when I said I'd call!" He stretched, felt his eyes close, then smiled to himself. No one had questioned him as to his whereabouts. He had simply reported that he'd found a break in the fence and repaired it. The truth. Nothing but the truth.

Just not the whole truth about his exciting day.

The rhythmic sound of horse's hooves and the entrance of a servant early the next morning interrupted the Sterling family breakfast. "Senor Tim, a vaquero from La Casa del Sol wishes to see you."

Tim felt a spurt of alarm. "Tell him to wait." He cut a piece of sausage and put it in his mouth. Funny. It tasted like sawdust.

"He says he must see you," the servant insisted. "That it is *importante.*"

Matt set down his coffee cup. "Are you sure he wants to see Tim?"

"Sí."

"Oh all right." Tim got up and started out. Matt and Sarah followed. *Great. I don't know what this is about, but the last thing I want is an audience. Besides, once word gets out — and there's no chance it won't — that I rescued the senorita, I won't be able to ride into town without getting ribbed.*

"No need for the rest of you to come," he protested.

"You can't know that," Matt retorted.

With a sigh of resignation, Tim marched out the front door and onto the wide porch. When he walked down the steps, a Mexican rider doffed his huge sombrero and slid from his horse's back.

"You are Senor Timothy Sterling?"

"I am."

The man held out a package. "Senor Montoya wishes you to have this."

Tim felt his ears burn. Not only would the cat soon be out of the bag, but there was no hope of escaping the consequences.

"You must open the package," the vaquero said. "Senor Montoya gave me orders." He crossed his arms over his chest and waited.

"What's this all about?" Matt demanded.

"Nothing."

"Nothing? Don Fernando isn't in the habit of sending presents to us. Open it."

Tim removed the string and tore the paper from the package. He stared at a small buckskin pouch. What on earth . . . ? He loosened the drawstring and turned the pouch upside down. A piece of cloth and a stream of shining silver coins cascaded through his fingers.

Stone-cold, dead silence followed the *clink* of the silver hitting the hard ground. The worst rage Tim had ever felt rose and threatened to suffocate him. He scooped up the coins, stuffed them back in the pouch, and strode toward the vaquero. "Take them back." Was that hoarse voice really his? "Tell Don Fernando I don't want them."

The man's soot-black eyes filled with fright. He put his hands out to ward off Tim. "No, no! Senor Montoya will be *muy enojado*. His anger will know no bounds." He sprang to the saddle and rode off.

Tim watched him go. So this was how Don Fernando repaid a kindness to his daughter — by sending money. Was it an obvious attempt to humiliate him? An ugly thought attacked. Did Angel know what her father had done?

Tim's heart sank. She must have. The coins had been wrapped in the neckerchief he had used to bind her arm.

NINE

The clatter of racing hooves dwindled and died. Tim threw the coin-filled buckskin pouch to the ground as if it were a hissing snake and headed toward the corral.

Matt Sterling's voice cut into his blind rage and stopped Tim in his tracks. "All right, Timothy. What is this all about?"

He spun on one boot heel and glared at Matt. "I shoulda just left her out there instead of setting myself up to get insulted."

Sarah ran down the steps, face filled with concern. She grabbed his arm and shook it. "What are you talking about? You should have left who where?"

A fresh burst of anger hit Tim, and he pulled free. "Senorita Angelina Carmencita Olivera Montoya, that's who," he snapped. "She sneaked away from La Casa del Sol on an ornery cayuse, tried to ride bareback, and got thrown. I found her unconscious. When she roused, Blue and I packed her home." He pointed to the buckskin pouch, retraced his steps, and picked it up. "And this is the thanks I get."

Matt reached Tim in two long strides. "Just where do you think you're going?"

Tim grabbed the pouch and stuffed it in his shirt pocket. Every jingle of the coins infuriated him more. "To show Senor High-and-Mighty Montoya that I don't take pay for playing Good Samaritan to his so-called angel of a daughter."

"Hold up." Matt's face resembled a thundercloud ready to boom its worst.

"Don't tell me to turn the other cheek and forbid me to go, Matt," Tim blazed.

"Forbid you? I'm going with you." A curious glint crept into Matt's blue eyes. "Remember the saying, 'You can catch more flies with honey than with vinegar?'"

Tim glared. "So? I'm not trying to catch flies."

"So there's a better way to handle this than going off half-cocked." Matt laughed. "First I have to ask: Is Angel Montoya as beautiful as they say?"

"Yeah." It slipped out before Tim could bite his unruly tongue. "What's that got to do with anything?"

"Would you like to get better acquainted with her?"

Tim met Matt's penetrating gaze head-on. "At first I thought so. Not now."

"Why?" Sarah wanted to know. "Don't blame her for what Don Fernando did."

"The coins came wrapped in my neckerchief, didn't they?"

Sarah didn't give an inch. Her blue eyes darkened. "That doesn't mean she knew Don Fernando's plan. Give her the benefit of the doubt, and stop playing judge and jury. People are innocent until proven guilty. The don would naturally know it was your kerchief used to bind Angel's arm."

Hope jolted through Tim. "You think she didn't know?"

Sarah sniffed. "I think any girl capable of defying orders and riding off bareback on an untrustworthy horse would object to her father sending you money." She smirked. "I know I would!"

Tim took a deep breath, held it, and slowly blew it out. With it went some of his tension. "Judgment delayed," he muttered and produced a grin to hide his relief. From the time Tim saw his neckerchief, it had not only rankled but also puzzled him. It certainly didn't match the welcome in Angelina's face when she had nodded agreement to his saying he would call and check on her health.

"Good luck," Sarah called when Tim and Matt had saddled up and started out for the House of the Sun. "We want to remain good neighbors with Senor Montoya — and with his daughter."

A peal of laughter warned Tim of teasing ahead. So much for his keeping to himself that love's lightning had once again struck the range.

A shortcut to La Casa del Sol cut down on the riding time. Matt and Tim talked of everything but the upcoming interview until just before they reached the sprawling hacienda. Then Matt raised an eyebrow and said, "Looks peaceful enough so far. One thing, hothead. Give me the coins, and above all, let *me* do the talking."

Tim opened his mouth to protest then clamped it shut and handed over the pouch. He knew from past experiences that Matt could hold his own when it came to confrontations. Tim scowled. This meeting could well turn out to be just that.

Ten minutes later the Montoya's butler, resplendent in the scarlet sash and regalia of a Spanish servant, opened the front door of the hacienda. A maid in colorful garb hovered in the distance. Both were in

100

character with the great hall in which they stood.

A beautifully carved table held a mass of blooming flowers. Small balconies displayed bright embroideries over their railings. Curious casement windows, lacy ironwork grills, and a winding staircase added to the charm. *Beautiful,* Tim decided, *but too fancy for me. Everything shouts money. I'll take the Diamond S ranch house any day.*

Matt's voice broke into his comparisons. "We wish to see Senor Montoya."

I don't. I want to see Senorita Angel and find out if she was party to her father's doings. Tim squelched a chuckle. It would never do to blurt out something like that to the officious butler.

"Wait here, senors." The butler strutted down the hall, back straight as a ramrod.

Tim wanted to laugh at the man's air of self-importance. So might King Solomon's chief adviser, whoever he'd been, have conducted himself. A slight rustle at the top of the stairs caught Tim's attention. He glanced up.

Sunlight streamed through a stained-glass window and rested on Angel Montoya as if glad to have found something worthy of its caress. It painted the girl's soft white gown and bandaged left arm in shades of ruby red, emerald green, sapphire blue, and topaz yellow and turned her into a living mosaic.

Tim gulped. He had never seen anything more beautiful. The look of delight in Angel's lovely face increased his feeling that she couldn't have known of her father's attempts to reduce a kind deed to silver coins.

Angel paused for a moment with her right hand on the gleaming banister rail. "Senor Tim. Welcome. I did not expect you to come so soon."

Tim descended from the heights of happiness to the depths of despair. When she learned why they had come, would the welcome in her dark eyes turn to scorn?

Don Fernando stepped into the hall in front of Tim and Matt. "You wished to see me?"

The highest peak of El Capitan during winter in Yosemite was no icier than his voice. It rang from the rafters and echoed in Tim's ears. His gaze fell from the staircase to the don's chiseled features. Pure Castilian. Obviously proud of it.

"Yes." Matt held out the buckskin pouch. "My son and I wish to return this."

Don Fernando crossed his arms over his white shirtfront. His words fell like stones. "I am grateful for what he did, but I will not be indebted to any man."

Tim cast a furtive glance at Matt. Would he back down?

Matt smiled, but his eyes flashed, and he continued to hold out the pouch. "We, sir, refuse to accept payment for a simple act of kindness to a neighbor." When Don Fernando just stared, Matt laid the pouch on the flower-laden table.

For a moment, Tim thought the hacendado would explode. But before he could speak, Angel ran down the stairs. Her face was whiter than her dress when she clutched his arm. "Papá, surely you didn't offer Senor Sterling *money* for bringing me home!"

"This is none of your affair, Angelina. Go to your room immediately."

Head drooping, she cast Tim a glance so filled with shame and apology that he wanted to give the haughty senor a kick in the seat of his immaculate black pants and send him flying down the hall. Tim took a step forward, but Matt's iron grip on his arm halted him. So did Matt's next words.

"We have no desire to make you feel in our debt. If you wish to repay Timothy, you will allow him to call on your daughter now and then — perhaps take her riding."

Don Fernando's thin lips parted, but Matt went on in the same bland tone, as if what he was suggesting would be the perfect solution for his stubborn opponent.

"They would, of course, be properly chaperoned. My wife, sister, and sister-in-law would all be more than happy to accompany them."

Tim writhed. Just what he didn't need: Sarah, Dori, or Ellie trotting along with him and Angel. On the other hand, what little chance he had of seeing the girl who now stood partway up the staircase would depend on it. He saw joy replace the sadness in Angel's face and caught the tiny nod she gave him from behind her father's rigid back.

Tim held his breath until he grew light-headed and had to cautiously let it out. It felt like an hour before a muscle twitched in the don's cheek and he drew himself to his full imposing height.

"I shall consider this matter and inform you of my decision," he said at last. "Now, you must come to the patio for a cool drink before returning to the Diamond S."

Once more Tim smothered a grin. Despite having been bested, or at least having the altercation end in an uneasy draw, Don Fernando appeared to have not lost one shred of his dignity.

He remained the perfect host when they

gathered in the courtyard. Even though Angel didn't join them, Tim enjoyed the scent of brightly blooming flowers, many in huge containers, the cool spray from the fountain, and the caroling of birds in the shady bushes. Most of all, he delighted in the delicious fruit lemonade and Mexican wedding cookies.

Tim helped himself to a second cookie and blurted out, "These are almost as good as Solita's." He felt his face flame and wished he could crawl into a hole, but Don Fernando's impassive features broke into a gleaming smile.

"I fear no one can ever make *cuernitos* as good as those prepared by your Solita. If it were not against the law, I would be tempted to kidnap her." He laughed. "Even I am not that brave. It would start a range war, and that we do not want."

Tim's mouth dropped open. It was the first time during their visit that he'd seen anything likable about the don. He wanted to assure their host that Angelina would be safe if allowed to ride with those from the Diamond S but hastily reconsidered. Best quit while he might be a little ahead of the game. One false move could mean losing what ground Matt may have gained.

A spurt of admiration filled Tim. How

clever for Matt to use the "soft answer turn-eth away wrath" approach. He had refused to bow to Don Fernando but had cleverly offered the proud man a way to save face.

Angel didn't appear while the Sterlings remained. But before they mounted for the long ride home, something drew Tim's gaze upward. Angel smiled down at him through an open casement window on the upper floor. As he watched, she looked both ways, apparently to make sure she was not ob-served. A split second later, a white handker-chief fluttered behind the iron grillwork then disappeared.

The effect of that farewell wave warmed Tim's heart all the way back to the Dia-mond S. He listened to Matt congratulate himself on how the interview had gone but only smiled. He brushed off Matt's remarks concerning "smitten young cowboys who didn't believe in love at first sight" the way he would brush off a pesky mosquito. Tim even pushed away the thought of teasing he'd be in for.

Right now, nothing mattered except that Angelina Carmencita Olivera Montoya had smiled down on him and waved.

TEN

Angel Montoya clutched her lacy white handkerchief in sweaty fingers and shrank back from the window without waiting to see if Tim responded to its flutter. "If Papá catches me waving farewell, I'll be in for another stormy session," she whispered. Memory of the scolding she had received for riding out alone sent heat to her face. So did the recent interview with the Sterlings.

Angel hurried into her bathroom and splashed cold water on her burning face. She patted her cheeks dry with a linen towel, but it did not cool the rebellion running through her veins like liquid fire.

"How could Papá send money to Senor Timothy for rescuing me?" she demanded of her reflection in the large framed mirror between two sconces. She stared into the image's dark eyes. Red patches remained on the cheekbones in spite of the cold water treatment.

A tap at the door was followed by a troubled, "Senorita, are you ill?"

"No." Angel stepped back into her bedroom and smiled at Conchita. She noted that her friend grew prettier every day, although trouble now showed in her smooth, brown face. "I'm angry and ashamed and excited and —" She broke off. "Conchita, how do you know if you are in love?"

Conchita's eyes opened wide. She crossed her arms over her embroidered white blouse, which set off her dark beauty. Its dainty ruffles swelled with her quick intake of breath. "You know in here." She hugged herself. "The first time I saw Emilio, I prayed that Dios might let me find favor with him." Mischief sparkled in her eyes. "I think perhaps you may have felt that way when Senor Sterling carried you home on his strong caballo."

Conchita's comment sent a fresh rush of warmth through Angel. It also brought back the feeling of security she had experienced while in her rescuer's arms, as if nothing could harm her. *Don't be foolish,* she told herself. *It's just that no man except Papá has ever held you so.*

A little voice inside jeered, *Then why is it*

108

that even the memory makes you tingle?

Determined to silence the annoying reminder, Angel plopped down on the window seat and motioned Conchita to a chair. "Don't you want to know why I am angry and ashamed and excited?"

"Sí." The little maid sat wide-eyed while Angel told of the Sterlings' visit.

"Papá is proud, but others also have pride," Angel choked out. Her anger lessened, and a faint giggle escaped. "You should have seen Papá's face when Senor Matthew Sterling said, 'We, sir, refuse to accept payment for a simple act of kindness to a neighbor' and laid the pouch filled with coins on the table."

Conchita gasped. "What did your father do?"

Angel squirmed. "I protested and —"

"With callers present?" Conchita looked appalled.

The enormity of her actions hit Angel fully for the first time. "Sí. I was so ashamed of what he had done, I did not stop to think. He told me it was not my affair and ordered me to go to my room."

Conchita shook her head, clearly puzzled. "Angry and ashamed I understand, but why are you excited?"

The same thrill that had soared through

Angel when she stood on the staircase came back a hundredfold. "Senor Sterling told Papá if he did not wish to be indebted he would permit Senor Timothy to call. Perhaps even permit me to ride with him, chaperoned by one of the senoras from the Diamond S."

Conchita couldn't have sounded more shocked if Angel had announced they were leaving La Casa del Sol forever. "Do you think Don Fernando will allow such a thing?"

"I do not know." Angel clasped her friend's hand and whispered so low Conchita bent forward to hear her. "I pray it will be so."

"Then I also shall pray."

The deep tones of the chapel bell calling the faithful to worship ended the conversation, but in the days that followed, Angel chafed at the bit and waited for her father's decision. No matter how often she told herself that Tim was occupying a far too prominent place in her thoughts, she couldn't put the tall cowboy out of her mind. Or the concern in his brown eyes and the tender way he had cared for her.

Not until all soreness had left Angel's arm did Papá send word for Tim and the senoras from the Diamond S to call. All three came:

Matt's wife, Sarah; his sister, Dori; and Tim's sister, Ellie. Papá was his usual courteous self, but Angel saw the way he studied the visitors. The women appeared not to notice but kept up a lively conversation about the charm of the hacienda and how nice it must be for Don Fernando to have Angel home again. She studiously avoided looking at Tim except for an occasional glance. If he was nervous, he didn't show it, but neither did he speak except when spoken to.

Only one slight hitch occurred during the visit. Dori's blue eyes flashed with fun when, in parting, she told Papá, "It is said that Angelina is not only the apple of your eye but also the whole orchard."

He visibly stiffened then nodded. "True, and she requires the same care."

Tim glared at his sister-in-law and took her arm. "We really must be going." He turned to Papá. "May we hope to have the pleasure of your daughter's company on a ride in the near future? Senorita Conchita as well, if she wishes."

"Please do," Sarah put in. "We would love to get to know Angelina better." Dori and Ellie murmured agreement.

Papá fitted his fingertips together and hesitated so long that Angel clenched her

111

hands until her nails bit into the palms. At last he said with obvious reluctance, "She may go tomorrow afternoon. I leave for San Francisco in the morning." He looked from face to face. "See that she is well taken care of." He sounded so haughty that Angel cringed, but Tim rose to the occasion.

"As if she were our own," he promised. "Until tomorrow, senorita."

Angel curtseyed and hoped her anticipation of the outing didn't show. But when she and her father were alone in the great hall, she laid her hand on his fine broadcloth coat sleeve. "Gracias, Papá." She wrinkled her forehead, and a niggling doubt diminished her happiness. "Why did you not tell me you were going to San Francisco?"

He patted her hand. "Something important has arisen. A matter I need to examine thoroughly." He paused and frowned. "I do not like to leave you without a duenna, but there was no time to find someone suitable, and I shall not be gone long. Besides, our servants are faithful, and Father Alfonso is steady as a rock. You are to consult with him should anything trouble you."

Pleasure over being left unchaperoned flowed through Angel. "I shall." She stood on tiptoe and kissed her father's cheek, then scampered upstairs to tell Conchita the latest news. Yet all the while the two girls rejoiced, something niggled at Angel's mind. Why this unexpected trip to San Francisco? Why had her father not insisted she go with him? Except for the time needed to run the hacienda, she'd seldom been out of his sight since she returned to the House of the Sun.

Early the next morning, Angel waved good-bye to her father from the front steps of the hacienda. Seated in a shining buggy with Juan at the reins, he made an imposing figure. Pride at being his daughter made Angel smile.

"I left instructions for you on my desk in the study, querida. Follow them. I shall return in a few days."

"Sí." She watched him ride out of sight then slowly walked to the study. Even though she knew a host of servants remained, the house had a hollow feel — as if lonely without the presence of the patrón. The reason why her father had left so quickly and avoided telling her the purpose of his trip continued to haunt her. It was so unlike him that it made Angel uneasy.

She reached the study and found the instructions, but they didn't solve the mystery. They contained little more than household reminders, things Angel already knew. Her father held strictly ornamental

113

girls in high contempt.

"You will be like my Carmencita," he had told Angel shortly after they had come home from San Francisco. "She kept her dainty fingers on the pulse of La Casa del Sol." A look of reminiscence softened his austere features. "She also wasn't above turning her hand to whatever needed doing." He frowned. "I don't suppose you learned to cook at the Garcias'. Tía Guadalupe would think it beneath your station."

"I can cook," she confessed. "Sometimes the nuns at the convent allowed me to help in the kitchen when I teased to do so."

"*Bueno!*" Laughter brightened his face. "Dios forbid that we should one day lose our hacienda and become peones, but if so, you can make the tortillas and tamales to sell in the marketplace."

She smirked. "They would be good ones, too."

He looked surprised. "But of course. Anything a Montoya does is done well."

"The hacienda isn't really in trouble, is it?" Angel inquired.

Papá shook his head. "No, yet things could change. Sickness among the cattle sometimes sweeps the range." A shadow crossed his face. "One cow with anthrax can infect a whole herd, and all must be destroyed. Horses, pigs, dogs, cats, goats, even wildlife can catch anthrax. But let us not talk of sad things." He straightened and smiled at her. "Our animals are healthy, and so are those of our neighbors. Now, when will you show me how well you can cook?"

Glad to have the subject of sickness closed, Angel tossed her head. "Not until I have more practice!"

In the following weeks, she and Conchita had invaded the cook's sacred precincts and become proficient in the art of cooking . . . so much so that her father teasingly threatened to fire the cook and put the girls in the kitchen.

Angel smiled at the memory and dropped the instructions back on the desk. The corner of a newspaper clipping peeked out from under the leather desk pad.

Angel stared. Her hand flew to her throat. A cold chill feathered her blood, and she found it hard to breathe. Surely this couldn't be what she feared, the source of her foreboding! She forced her trembling fingers to pull out the clipping.

Ramon Chavez's face stared up at her, arrogant and repulsive.

Angel's heart pounded until she felt it would burst from her chest. She tottered and would have fallen if she hadn't clutched at the edge of the desk. She swallowed hard to keep back nausea. Her father's words pounded in her mind: *Something important has arisen. A matter I need to examine thoroughly. I do not like to leave you without a duenna, but there was no time to find someone suitable.*

If Papá had been going on hacienda business he would have said so. Suspicion grew. Did the trip have to do with her father's determination to arrange a marriage for her with Chavez? Papá had said no more about it since Tía Guadalupe's letter first came. Angel had hoped her vehement protest against Chavez as a suitor had softened her father's heart.

"I shall never marry that man," she vowed.

The sound of her voice brought strength. She lifted the desk pad in search of an explanation as to why Papá had left in such haste. An embossed envelope addressed in Tía's writing lay like a coiled rattlesnake awaiting its victim. She snatched it up and removed the single sheet of monogrammed stationery.

If you wish to secure Senor Chavez for Angelina, come immediately. Although attracted by her picture, he grows impatient. The city is filled with those eager

116

to become his bride. I fear that any delay on your part may prove to be fatal.

"Fatal to me." A sob tore through Angel. Her fingers itched to shred the letter and clipping. She dared not. Doing so would anger her father and make things worse, if that was possible. Tucking the offensive material back under the desk pad, she fled to the sanctuary of her room.

ELEVEN

Angelina tapped on Conchita's door, wanting nothing more than to throw herself into her friend's arms and receive comfort. The door remained closed. Evidently Conchita was busy elsewhere in the hacienda.

Angel sank to her bed and beat her fists against the pillows. *Oh Mamá, if you were only here! Surely you would not make me marry Senor Chavez.* Her silent plea rang in her ears like a death knell. Mamá was not here. Who could she turn to?

Her father's admonition that *"Father Alfonso is steady as a rock. You are to consult with him should anything trouble you"* popped into Angel's mind. She sprang from her bed, flew down the winding staircase, and walked to the hacienda chapel. Once inside, she slipped into a pew and knelt on the rich carpet. Hoping for peace, she let the silence surround her. Peace eluded her — as it had eluded her father all through his years of

118

desperate searching. A vision of the sadness in his dark eyes and voice rose before Angel. If such a devout man could not find peace in spite of lighting hundreds of candles and confessing his sins to Father Alfonso, what hope was there for her?

She pushed aside her doubts. She would find peace. She must. But how?

A hand gently touched her shoulder. "My daughter, what troubles you? Have you come to confess?"

Angel shrank from the idea. Shame ran through her veins. How could she confess she would rather die than enter an arranged marriage, especially to Ramon Chavez? Or that even though she had only seen Timothy Sterling twice, her traitorous heart yearned for the tall cowboy? Father Alfonso would be horrified. Although compelled to never disclose what he heard in confessionals, the weight of her secret would rest heavily on his aged shoulders.

Angel took a deep breath and looked up into his kindly brown face. "I did not come to confess. I have a question." She clasped her hands to still their trembling. "How far must one go in order not to dishonor one's parents?"

He crossed his arms over his cassock and looked appalled. "I am surprised at you,

Angelina. After all your studies at the convent, you ask me this? You certainly must have been taught that we are commanded to obey our parents."

Angel's heart felt as if it had dropped to her toes. "Even when forced to do something that will take the joy from life forever?" Her voice quavered.

His jaw set. "Joy is found in duty and obedience. Consider that well; then return and make your confession. I do not know what it is you refer to, but it is dangerous to have rebellion in your heart." Father Alfonso strode past her to the front of the chapel and vanished through a door behind the altar, leaving Angel to stare after him and wish she had never come home to the House of the Sun.

After a long time, Angel stood and made her way back to the house, which felt more like a prison than ever. Her feet dragged as she trudged up the stairs. When she came to her room, the door flew open. Conchita stood there, dressed in riding clothes and with concern in her eyes. She carried a plate containing a sandwich and a crystal goblet filled with milk.

"Where have you been? The clock has struck twelve. You have not eaten and are not ready for the guests who will arrive soon. Let me help you." She turned Angel around and began unbuttoning the tiny buttons on the back of her gown.

Angel gasped. Incredible as it seemed, discovery of Tía's letter had made her forget that Timothy and a chaperone were coming to take her and Conchita riding. For a split second she toyed with the idea of making an excuse not to go. How could she ride and pretend to enjoy herself while a heavy cloud of misery hung over her? On the other hand, how could she quench the excitement sparkling in Conchita's eyes?

Doing so would be unkind and foolish, a little voice whispered. *Besides, this may be your only chance to ride with Senor Timothy. If you give it up you are already beaten.*

Montoya pride swelled. Although the sandwich held no appeal and she could only drink half of the milk, Angel rallied. She was dressed and ready by the time Tim and Sarah Sterling arrived. His look of admiration and something else she could not define repaid her efforts.

At first they rode four abreast, but Angel wanted to gallop. She wanted to escape the bittersweet feeling that warned her that this first ride might also be their last. Did she dare suggest it?

Sarah's melodious voice cut into Angel's

reflections. "Tim, Blue acts like he needs a good run. So does White Woman. Why don't you and the senorita race to that cluster of trees?" She pointed to a stand of giant oaks almost out of sight. "Conchita and I will poke along and get better acquainted, if that is all right with her."

Conchita sent Angel a look of mischief. But instead of giggling, as Angel expected, she remained solemn. "Sí, Senora Sterling." She patted her horse. "My amiga knows I like to — what you say — poke along."

Tim waited until White Woman moved up beside Blue. "Ready?"

"Ready." Angel bent low in the saddle and clamped her legs like a vise to her horse's sides. "Go, Blanca!" White Woman responded with a gigantic leap that put her a full length ahead of Blue.

Not for long. With a "Ya-hoo! See you at the oaks!" Tim goaded his mount into a ground-swallowing run that brought them neck and neck with Angel and White Woman. They remained that way until just short of the designated end of the course. Then Tim let out another cowboy yell. His powerful roan gave a final, mighty spring and won the impromptu race by half a length.

Angel reined in White Woman and slid

from the saddle without waiting for Tim's help. The feel of the wind in her face and the exhilaration of the ride had left her breathless. "That was good." She sank to the ground, and Tim followed.

"Yes. God and Don Fernando willing, we can have many other rides." He sounded delighted at the prospect.

Angel's restored spirits crashed to the ground. "I fear it cannot be." She looked away from him and tried to hold back tears.

He looked surprised. "Why not? Your father allowed you to come today."

Tell him. Tell him that unless you are mightily mistaken, you are the same as betrothed.

Angel could not. Instead she blurted out, "When you are troubled, what do you do?"

"Go to my Father."

"Do you confess to Senor Matthew and receive pardon?" she asked.

Tim shook his head. The sweetest smile she had ever seen on a man's face lighted his features. "Matt is a wonderful earthly father, but I go straight to my heavenly Father. God is the One who holds forgiveness and offers help in time of trouble."

Angel stared. Never had she seen anyone whose face glowed like Tim's. Her father's story of the former bandido who came to La Casa del Sol with the message that God loved Don Fernando and offered him peace sprang to her mind. He had added, *"Senor. We have both been without hope. God had mercy on me. He longs to do the same for you."*

Angel remembered her father's expression when he said, *"Something prevented me from having the presumptuous rider thrown off the hacienda. I do not understand why the memory of his face rode with me for weeks. . . . In spite of his rough clothing and ways, he wore peace like a cloak. Peace I desperately needed and had not found."*

Angel had not fully understood at the time. Now she did. Timothy Sterling wore that same cloak of peace. Her heart lurched. If only she could find it and share it with her father!

"Angel, what makes you so sad?" Tim placed one hand over her small gloved one. "It hurts me to see you like this."

The genuine concern in his voice broke through the wall of family loyalty Angel had observed since childhood. She bowed her head. Tears gushed. "I fear Papá has gone to arrange my marriage with a rich Mexican hacendado old enough to be my father. Almost old enough to be my grandfather!"

Tim's hand tightened. "Surely you don't want to marry such a man!"

Angel shuddered. "I would rather lie cold and dead than to become his wife, but how can I disobey Papá?" She didn't wait for a reply. "This morning I went to the chapel and talked with Father Alfonso. He said we are commanded to obey our parents, even if it takes the joy from life. He said joy comes from duty and obedience and that it is dangerous for me to have rebellion in my heart."

When Tim did not reply, Angel stole a glance at him. He sat with bowed head. His lips moved in what she suspected was silent prayer. Had he gone to his heavenly Father on her behalf? She felt warmth rise from the collar of her starched white blouse. In all her imaginings, she had never expected to meet a man like this.

At last Tim opened his eyes and looked into hers. "It is true that we are commanded to obey our parents. Colossians 3:20 in the holy Bible makes this clear: 'Children, obey your parents in all things: for this is well pleasing unto the Lord.' We must always be faithful and do those things that please Him."

A wave of nausea rose, so strong Angel feared she would choke. She freed her hand from the comforting clasp that had proved to be against her, along with the rest of the world. "Obey in all things? Then Father Alfonso is right. I must marry without love, or dishonor my father." She leaped to her feet and started toward White Woman.

Tim rose. "Wait, Angel. There's more."

Was that bitter laugh her own? She whirled toward Tim, whose steady gaze met hers without flinching or apology. "I don't want to hear anything else."

"You must," he said. "There is more to the passage. The apostle Paul warns in the very next verse, 'Fathers, provoke not your children to anger, lest they be discouraged.' That lays a heavy responsibility on Don Fernando as well as on you."

Hope no larger than a firefly flickered in Angel's heart, but disbelief extinguished it. "If this is so, why did Father Alfonso not tell me?"

Compassion flowed from Tim's eyes. "It is not for me to judge. I only know that the words of the holy Bible are true." He looked across to the hazy hills barely visible from where they stood. His expression made Angel suspect that he was seeing far more than parched grass and grazing cattle in the distance.

"More than ten years ago, God rescued my sister, Ellie, and me from a life of misery. Some time later I asked Jesus to be my Trailmate and live in my heart. Since then His presence is with me; I am never alone. He has rescued me from danger many times." A glorious smile appeared, and Tim exclaimed, "He even taught me to forgive those who did Ellie and me dirt!"

Angel sucked in a great breath but slowly exhaled when Tim continued.

"God heals broken hearts and gives peace. No problem is too big for Him, but you have to ask. Jesus told those who followed Him, 'Ask, and it shall be given you; seek, and ye shall find; knock, and it shall be opened unto you: For every one that asketh receiveth; and he that seeketh findeth; and to him that knocketh it shall be opened.' "

Once more her father's voice echoed in Angel's mind. *I call myself loco for hoping to one day find peace. Yet how can a man live without hope?"*

Tim's words sank deep into Angel's aching heart. Was it possible that all she and her father had to do was to ask? Doubt assailed her. It seemed too simple. If only she could find out more about it!

Her wish died a-borning. The steady *clip-clop* of horses and Sarah and Conchita's laughter heralded their arrival and put an end to private conversation. Yet all the way back to the House of the Sun, Angel — like

Mary of old — pondered many things in her heart and wondered if what Tim said could really be true.

TWELVE

Angel slid from the saddle and turned Blanca over to a vaquero at the hacienda corral, then watched Tim and Sarah Sterling ride away. Disappointment and regret surged through her. If only Sarah and Conchita had not reached the stand of oaks when they did! Perhaps Senor Timothy would have explained why he and the bandido who came to her father had peace when she and her father did not. What would it be like to have *Jesús* for a Trailmate? To never feel alone and helpless as she often did, especially since she had learned of her father's plan to arrange her betrothal.

Tim had said no problem was too big for God. Angel sighed. Her predicament seemed too huge even for Him. If she refused Ramon Chavez or another suitor Papá chose, would she be cast out of her father's house? Weariness fell over her like a water-soaked blanket. All she wanted was a bath and the comfort of her bed.

"Come, Conchita," she called.

Her friend sent a pleading look toward her then shook her head at Emilio Sanchez, who had helped her dismount. The wrangler said something too low for Angel to catch. Tears streamed when Conchita hurried to answer Angelina's summons. Her forlorn expression turned Angel's attention from her own troubles. She laid an arm over the little maid's shaking shoulders. "What is it?"

Emilio strode toward them. Conchita shrank against Angel.

Angel glared at Emilio. "Why did you make her cry?" Then she noticed the misery in the young man's eyes, the droop of his usually smiling lips.

"Por favor, may I speak with you, senorita? I have very bad news." The pain in his voice cooled Angel's anger. She glanced at the circle of gaping vaqueros and motioned Emilio to follow her. Arm still around Conchita, she led them a little distance away to where they could have privacy.

Emilio held out a slip of paper. "A *telegrama* came. Mamá is very sick in *México*. She calls for me." He cast Conchita a look so filled with love and despair that Angel ached for him. "But how can I leave my

130

beautiful Conchita? I do not know when I shall return. *Mi familia* will need me." He gulped and placed one hand over his heart. "If the blessed Senorita Angel will allow us to stand before the padre, Conchita will become *mi esposa* and go with me."

Angel felt like she'd been kicked by a mule. "*Your wife?* Emilio, do you know what you are asking?"

"Sí." He bowed until his shining black hair touched the ground then proudly raised his head. "I plead for the hand of the one I love."

Angel turned from the beseeching dark eyes, feeling she held the fate of all three of them in her gloved fingers. She dropped her arm from Conchita's shoulders and stepped back. "Conchita, is this what you want? To leave La Casa del Sol and go with Emilio?" Her voice trembled. What would she do without Conchita?

"How can I leave you?" Conchita wailed, fingers over her wet face. "But how can I tell Emilio *adios* and perhaps never see him again?"

Her friend's heartfelt cry of love did what nothing else could have done. Angel gathered Conchita back into her arms and spoke over the girl's shoulder to Emilio. "I cannot give permission for such a plan, but I will

131

send word to my father. You must remain here until we receive a reply."

"Sí." Emilio seized her hand, something Angel knew he would never do except in a time of great emotion. He gripped it until Angel winced, and then he burst out, *"¡Vaya con Dios!"*

Desolation built inside Angel, and she fought tears. If Conchita left and Papá remained determined to carry out his plan, she would need God with her more than ever.

The thought recurred again and again during the next few hours. Angel dispatched a rider to Madera on one of the fastest of the Montoya horses. She gave him orders to wait for an answer to her telegram explaining the situation. She closed with:

CONCHITA AND EMILIO LOVE EACH OTHER *Stop* I SHALL MISS HER BUT PRAY THAT YOU WILL ALLOW THEM TO WED *Stop*

Permission came back almost immediately. Early the next morning, the couple stood before Father Alfonso and took their vows. Angel had produced a white gown and mantilla for Conchita that set off her dark beauty. Ever the dandy, Emilio was resplendent in a charro outfit: silver decorations, tight trousers, ruffled shirt, and short jacket. When he helped his bride into the carriage that would take them to Madera to catch the train, he carried a highly decorated sombrero.

Angel did not go to the station. She feared she might break down when telling Conchita good-bye. Pride refused to allow her to become a spectacle to the curious crowd that attended the coming and going of the train. It might be months or even years before she and Conchita met again. Perhaps never.

Angel swallowed the tumbleweed-sized lump in her throat, forced a smile, and held it there until the carriage with Emilio and his happy but tearful bride vanished in the distance. Then she slowly made her way from the chapel back to the main house, feeling more alone than she had ever been in her life.

Seeking solitude, Angel dragged herself into the courtyard and sat down in the shade of a tree. She relived the past few hours. A bitter laugh escaped. "This simple ceremony is nothing compared with the pomp and circumstance of Angelina Carmencita Olivera Montoya's wedding. Guests will be summoned from far and near. They will come prepared to stay for many days of fiesta." She dropped her head into her hands. "Alas, there will be no love such as Conchita and Emilio have." Envy for the little maid brought hot tears. "Emilio is only a horse wrangler, but he loves Conchita with all his heart. He will make her happy, for she loves him enough to leave all she knows and go with him."

A nearby bird burst into song. Another joined in, then another, until the air rang as if in tribute to the beautiful world in which they lived. The music only made Angel's heart ache more. "There will be no songs in my life if Papá has his way," she whispered. "Never could Ramon Chavez be like Emilio and bring me joy. Or make me willing to forsake everything and go where he leads as Conchita has done."

As you would do if you became Timothy Sterling's bride.

The words clanged in Angel's mind. She furtively glanced both ways to make sure she had not spoken aloud and been overheard. Closing her eyes, she remembered every moment she had spent with the Diamond S cowboy. She reveled in the memories. Conchita's wedding had intensified her growing love for the man who first rescued her, then spoke new and strange things. How different her wedding day would be if Timothy Sterling waited for her at the altar instead of the rich Mexican hacendado!

The thought set her heart thumping, but hot tears followed. "Even if there were no Ramon Chavez, there would be others like him," she choked out. "Papá would never permit me to marry a cowboy. Not even the son of Senor Matthew Sterling, with all his lands and cattle." She rose and trudged into the hacienda, unable to bear the continuing birdsongs. If only she could be free like the birds — free to fly away from the life required of her by years of tradition and her father's belief that he knew best.

One of the hardest things Timothy Sterling ever had to do was to ride away from La Casa del Sol and the unspoken appeal in Angelina Montoya's great dark eyes. How quickly the excitement of their impromptu race had fled with his impulsive words. Pain had replaced the joy in Angel's face, and her confession that she might already be betrothed made Tim shudder.

A prayer rose to his lips. "Lord, if Angel is truly promised to another, I have no right to feel the way I do. Yet she said she would rather lie cold and dead than marry the man her father has chosen. I feel like rushing to San Francisco and shaking the living daylights out of Don Fernando. What right has he to force his daughter into marriage with a man she fears?

"I pray that I answered her questions in the way You would have had me do. She is torn between love for her father and —"

Tim broke off. Had he gone loco? It was bigheaded to think that Angel returned the love that had struck him at their first meeting like a speeding arrow. Or was it? Her expressive face, the way rich color came and went in her smooth cheeks, even the manner in which she had appealed to him betrayed far more than a casual interest.

Sarah, who rode beside him and had remained quiet ever since they left the hacienda, broke into his reflections. "Tim, are you in love with Angelina?"

His hands tightened on Blue's reins. "Yes."

She gave a little cry. "Nothing can come of it, you know."

Tim stared at his sister. "It doesn't make any difference. Besides, God can move mountains."

Sarah's light-blue eyes teared up. "Don Fernando Montoya is pure granite. When it comes to his only child, he will be harder to budge than . . ." Her voice trailed off.

Tim forced his lips into a grin, reached over, and patted her gloved hands. "Don't worry. No man is bigger or more powerful than God."

"I know, but —"

"But nothing. I didn't ask to meet Angelina Carmencita Olivera Montoya and fall in love with her at first sight." Tim clenched his teeth. "Sarah, we need to pray for her and not worry about how I feel." He related his conversation with Angel. "She desperately needs to find peace. I hope what I told her helped."

"How did she respond?"

Tim shoved his Stetson back on his head and stared at his stepsister. "Like a drowning man clutching for anything he could find to save him. I wish you and Conchita hadn't ridden up when you did. There was so much more I could have told her."

After a long silence broken only by the *clip-clop* of the horses' hooves, Sarah said, "Perhaps it is best that we came when we did. The things you told her are new and strange to Angelina. She needs time to consider them." Sarah paused. "You must remember this. She worships God in a different way than we are accustomed to doing. We find answers for ourselves by reading the Bible and praying directly to God.

The Montoyas rely on the scriptures the priest chooses to read in Latin, through confession, and doing the penance he prescribes.

"I don't want to treat your feelings lightly, but we are warned not to be unequally yoked. No two people are more unequally yoked than you and Angel." Her voice turned shaky. "I don't want to see either of you hurt. I probably shouldn't say this, but I suspect Angelina has learned to care for you even in the short time she has known you. It shows in the softness of those dark eyes. But remember this: She is young, barely eighteen."

Hope soared. Past experience had taught Tim that Sarah never spoke lightly of things she discerned. "I am less than a year older," he reminded her.

Sarah shook her head. "You are years older than she is in life experiences. You have faced danger, even death, in your range work. You have learned to trust our heavenly Father in all things. Angelina has been sheltered, pampered, and brought up according to ways that are centuries old, including her sincere belief in a formal faith."

Sarah's concerned tone of voice and look of compassion sent Tim's high spirits packing. "You feel there is no hope for us?"

She shook her head. "Not unless God chooses to tear down the wall between you, and it is high. Why don't you talk with Josh? Remember the difficulties he and Ellie faced in their courtship because of the Stanhopes' position in high society? Your situation is not the same, but he will understand."

"I appreciate your trying to help, Sarah, but keep mum. I need to work this out with God." Tim twisted his lips into a crooked grin. "Like I told Angel, there's nothing too big for Him to handle, but boy, this is one tough problem to dump on His doorstep!"

Tim touched his heels to Blue's flanks and leaned forward, urging his horse into a gallop. But he could not outrun the trouble that had come into his life when he first discovered Angel Montoya lying unconscious in the shade of the giant oak.

THIRTEEN

The day after Emilio and Conchita left La Casa del Sol, a telegram arrived from San Francisco. Angelina's fingers shook when she tore it open. She glanced at the message and felt her last spark of hope flicker and die.

ARRANGEMENTS COMPLETE *Stop* WILL BE HOME TOMORROW *Stop* READY GUEST CHAMBER FOR SENOR CHAVEZ *Stop*

Summoning every ounce of strength she could muster, Angel bit her lip and held back the dizziness that threatened to send her crashing to the floor. Once she regained control of herself, she called for the servants and informed them of their master's return.

"Prepare the rooms reserved for our most important visitors," she said. "Papá is bringing a guest." Yet all the time Angel gave the orders, her heart protested, *If I had my way, Senor Chavez would be given lodging with the pigs or chickens, not welcomed as an honored guest.*

The thought of the hacendado being forced to bed down with farm animals made Angel smile in spite of feeling that tears flowed from her hurting heart. But when she surveyed the gorgeous guest chamber adorned with rich tapestries and filled with flowers, the smile fled. If her father had truly betrothed her to Ramon Chavez, this would be her last night of real freedom.

When twilight fell, Angel sought refuge in her room. Instead of lighting a lamp, she curled up on the cushioned window seat and stared through the open window into the night sky. Great clusters of stars and a round yellow moon made the courtyard below as light as day. Wild thoughts raced through Angel's mind. If only she had somewhere to go, someone to turn to! The House of the Sun no longer held sunlight for her. The overwhelming desire to escape brought her to her feet. What if she were to mount White Woman right now and ride away?

"I have no one," she told the breeze that danced in through her window and cooled her hot face. "Father Alfonso would reprimand me then report to Papá. Emilio and Conchita are far away. Sarah Sterling seemed kind, but would she dare give me sanctuary?" Hopelessness raged through Angel's body. Her father's fury would know no bounds should any person attempt to interfere with his plans. She dared not expose anyone to the retribution he would surely deal out.

Angel sat down, crossed her arms on the windowsill, and leaned her aching head against them. She whispered the prayers she had been taught, but they did not still her restless spirit or make her feel less alone. In the silence that followed, broken only by a night bird's cry, Tim's words returned to her, soothing as crushed aloe vera leaves. *"I go straight to my heavenly Father. God is the One who holds forgiveness and offers help in time of trouble. . . . I asked Jesus to be my Trailmate. . . . His presence is with me; I am never alone. . . . Ask and ye shall receive. . . ."*

Angel raised her tear-wet face toward the heavens. "Please. Help me." She waited, not knowing what to expect. No thunderbolt came. No message of hope flashed across the sky like a comet in its fiery course. No promise that tomorrow her problems would all be solved beat into Angel's brain. Yet after a time, comfort came.

With a whispered, "Gracias," Angel left the window seat and crawled into bed. Propped against her pillows, she continued to gaze out at the starry sky. But even its glory was no match for the stress of the day. Five minutes later she fell into the deepest sleep she had known since her father left for San Francisco.

Angel awakened to the sound of a rooster crowing in the new day. Rested and refreshed, she bounded out of bed and to her window. Her father's terse message shot into her mind: *Arrangements complete.* The slight comfort she had known the previous night took flight. "Before darkness falls, Papá and Senor Chavez will arrive," she murmured. "Life will never again be the same, and there is nothing I can do."

She flung herself back among her lacy pillows but sat up the next moment and squared her shoulders. "Angelina Carmencita Olivera Montoya, where is your pride?" she demanded. "Stop this sniveling, and conduct yourself as a woman. And never, *ever* show Ramon Chavez that you fear him." She glanced at the wardrobe that housed her vast array of clothing and set her lips in a determined line. "This is not a joyous occasion. Do not dress like it is," she admonished herself.

Fortified by the scolding, Angel hurried to her wardrobe. She thrust aside yellow gowns and white, green, blue, pink, red, and orchid. At last she pulled out a new black frock and held it up to her body. A quick look in the mirror reassured her. Row after row of tiny, lace-edged ruffles cascaded from the modestly rounded neckline to her bare feet. She snatched up a fan of magnificent black plumes. It would hide the trembling of her lace-mitted hands when in the presence of Senor Chavez.

A second glance brought a triumphant smile. Not even Papá could find fault with the costume, although her choice to wear black might well bring a scowl of disapproval. Angel's heartbeat quickened. What if he reproved her before the visitor? It would be more than she could bear to have the unwelcome suitor see her humiliated.

The thought haunted her while she hung the dress back in its place, slipped into a house gown, and managed to choke down a few bites of breakfast. But long before she could reasonably expect her father and Chavez to arrive, Angel's nerves twanged like badly plucked guitar strings.

At last it was time to dress. Unwilling to

listen to chatter, Angel refused to summon a maid and instead donned the black dress without help. She perched on the window seat above the courtyard. When she heard the sound of carriage wheels, she leaned from her window and plucked a single rose, as white as her face in the mirror. Angel breathed in its perfume and nestled it against her shoulder — the lone concession to pleasing her father and still maintaining a bit of independence.

She caught up the plumy fan and stared at her mirrored image. Twin red spots burned in her pale cheeks. Her eyes glistened with unshed tears. Step by step she opened her door and swept down the staircase into the great hall, chin held high.

The front door swung open. Papá stepped into the hall and stood aside for his companion to enter. *"Bienvenido,* Senor Chavez. *Mi casa es su casa."*

Angel cringed. She recognized the polite greeting for guests, but somehow the innocent "My house is your house" took on new meaning, as if Papá were offering their home to Senor Chavez . . . permanently. She glanced at the visitor, who was even more repulsive in real life than in the newspaper image. When he looked around the richly furnished hall, an expression of unmistakable greed showed in Chavez's swarthy face. He licked his thick lips and fixed his gaze on Angel.

"Gracias. And this must be my betrothed."

A slight smile and the possession in his voice shattered the ice Angel felt forming around her body. Wed this man? *Never!* She fought for words. None came. *Say something, anything, to erase Ramon Chavez's gloating,* a little voice prompted.

Clutching her fan until her fingers ached, Angel groped for a reason that would stand up against her father's pride. A lie sprang to mind. Another, one that would set a barrier between her and Ramon Chavez forever. Angel curtseyed. The first lie rolled off her tongue as if she were accustomed to perjuring herself. "I am honored by your interest, senor." Honored? More like terrified and repulsed. "But I cannot marry you."

The hacendado's face looked shocked. He opened his mouth to speak, but Papá beat him to it.

"What is this, Angelina?" he thundered. "How dare you insult our guest?"

The habit of obedience and truthfulness made her falter, but the little voice encouraged: *Better to commit a sin than belong to Chavez.* Angel straightened to her full height and looked straight into the visitor's

146

contorted features.

"I do not mean to insult you, but I cannot marry you. I — I am thinking about entering a convent." Appalled by what she had done, Angel raised her fan high enough to cover her trembling lips. *Please, God, don't strike me dead for telling such a monstrous lie. I respect those who live inside cloistered walls, but I would shrivel and die.*

Chavez looked as if he might explode. He shook a fat finger in her father's face. "You brought me all the way here to be insulted like this?" he bellowed. His voice bounced off the high ceiling of the hall and echoed in Angel's ears. She looked from him to her father, hoping to find a gleam of sympathy in his dark eyes.

There was none.

"Go to your room, Angelina. I will speak with you later. Change your gown. This one makes you look like a crow." Papá turned back to Chavez and dropped an arm over his shoulders. "Come into my study, senor. This is all foolishness. Angelina has been sheltered and is young for her years."

Angel stumbled toward the stairs, cut to the heart and more humiliated than she had been in her entire life. Worse, she had lied. What had she gained? Nothing. Papá had not even taken her seriously.

In the temporary safety of her room, Angel tore off the scorned dress and bundled it onto the bed. The fan followed, black as the lies that repeated themselves in her brain. She rang for a maid. When the girl came, Angel pointed to the heap on the bed. "Take them away." Memory of her humiliation set her blood on fire. "Keep them if you like, but never let me see them again. They make me look like a crow."

Disbelief crept into the girl's eyes. "Your new gown? But senorita —"

"Take it and go!" Angel had never spoken so to a servant, but the gown and fan had grown unbearable in her sight.

The girl obeyed without another word.

For the second time that day, Angel examined her array of clothing. She passed by the rainbow of hues and reached for her favorite white frock. The next moment she dropped it as if the material burned her hands. "White is for purity," she whispered. "I have no right to wear it. White is also is for brides. I want no reminder of that now."

After much consideration she snatched an elegant, ice-blue brocade from its hanger, thankful that it buttoned from the high, stiff collar to a point below the waist. She would not require the help of a maid. Once dressed, Angel piled her hair high on her head in a different style than she usually wore. She added a jeweled comb, then sat down on the window seat to await her time of reckoning.

It came an hour later. When her father tapped at the door, Angel pinched her cheeks to add color, stood, and bade him enter.

Papá, more imposing than ever in formal dinner clothing, loomed over her. His gaze swept from the sparkling comb to the tips of her dainty blue slippers. The muscles of his face visibly relaxed. "You look more like your mother than ever."

The tenderness in his tone caught Angel off guard. She had fully expected him to demand an explanation, then chastise her severely. She ran to him and threw herself against him. Tears gushed.

Her father's arms tightened around her. "Do not cry, querida."

"I cannot help it. I am so sorry. I told you a terrible falsehood, Papá. I could never join a convent."

"I thought not." He gently pushed her back and looked deep into her eyes. "You dislike Senor Chavez so much it causes you to lie?"

Angel's head drooped. "Sí."

Her father sounded troubled when he

replied, "I do not understand. Senor admires you greatly and has much to offer. Perhaps it is because I have been too hasty in making arrangements and given you no time to get acquainted." His face brightened. "Do you wish for me to tell him there will be no formal announcement until he has been with us for a time?"

Angel bit her tongue to keep from blurting out that it would make no difference if Chavez stayed at La Casa del Sol for the rest of his life. Her heart belonged to a tall cowboy who wore peace like a garment. Yet Papá's suggestion was far more than she had expected. It gave her a reprieve. She nodded.

He rubbed his hands together. "Bueno." His teeth gleamed in a wide smile. "We have not yet had a celebration to welcome you home. We will make a fiesta and invite friends and neighbors from far and near."

Neighbors, including those from the Diamond S?

Angel's heartbeat quickened. At least one good thing would come from Ramon Chavez's visit: she would get to see Timothy Sterling again.

FOURTEEN

The thrum of guitars, click of castanets, and joyous sounds of horns greeted Timothy Sterling when he rode up to the House of the Sun on fiesta day. Tree branches dripped piñatas. Blindfolded children swarmed below and attacked the colorful papier-mâché creations with long poles. One, more successful than the others, hit hard enough to break a multi-colored donkey. It showered down sweetmeats and coins amidst the triumphant cries of the children.

Tim sniffed the enticing aroma of roasting meat coming from the whole steer spitted over a well-tended fire. "I can sure do with some grub." He dismounted and turned Blue over to a waiting vaquero who wore a smile wider than a crack in an overripe watermelon. "Is everyone in Madera here?" Tim asked.

The vaquero placed one hand over his heart. "Sí, senor. All come to honor our senorita." The joy in his brown face turned to sadness. He looked both ways as if afraid of being overheard and lowered his voice. "It is said the blessed Senorita Angel will soon leave us and wed the hacendado from México. I fear that the day she goes will be the day the sun no longer shines on La Casa del Sol and the little birds do not sing."

Tim's spirits plummeted. "Has the senorita's betrothal been announced?"

The vaquero shrugged one serape-covered shoulder and hitched his wide sombrero forward. "I think perhaps it will happen on this day." The picture of dejection, he trudged away, grumbling to himself and leading Blue.

Tim watched him go, wanting to snatch Blue's reins and ride away. No. Leaving would be cowardly. He was here. Here he would stay. Tim set his jaw. "So what if it's true, Lord?" he muttered. "I'm not going until I see and hear for myself." He squared his shoulders and began working his way through the crowd that spilled out of the open gates and into the shaded yard. He caught sight of Angel, surrounded by men and girls whose fiesta garb created an ever-changing kaleidoscope of color as they shifted patterns. Tim gaped. Angel's filmy, pale-yellow gown and white mantilla made her even more beautiful than he remembered.

How will she greet me? Tim wondered. His pulse raced. He quickened his steps — but came to an abrupt stop when a massive man elbowed his way through the laughing crowd around Angel and stepped to her side. His heavy black eyebrows and moustache concealed much of his face, but Tim took an instant dislike to the stranger. Angel's words rang in the cowboy's brain: *"I fear he has gone to arrange my marriage with a rich Mexican hacendado old enough to be my father. Almost old enough to be my grandfather!"*

Tim clenched his hands. Angels and devils did not unite, and Tim fancied he could see horns sprouting from Ramon Chavez's sleek head. The senor's expression when he looked down at Angel reminded Tim of the look he'd once seen in a rattlesnake's eyes just before he struck.

Hold it, Tim. Your love for Angel is probably clouding your judgment. Chavez may be shady, but that doesn't mean he's a rattlesnake. Or a devil. But if he is, God save her from a fate worse than death.

Tim took a deep breath and forced himself to slowly expel it. He raised his chin and started toward Angel, but a heavy hand on his shoulder spun him around. Sheriff Meade, who had been the law in Madera since before Tim came to the Diamond S, wore a scowl as black as Senor Chavez's moustache.

"Is that the yahoo Montoya aims to hitch Angel up to?" The scowl grew deeper.

"That's what I hear," Tim mumbled.

"Don't like his face." The sheriff scratched his ear and lowered his voice. "If he wasn't so duded up, he'd look good on a wanted poster."

"Not likely. Rumor has it he's such a bigwig that half of San Francisco is licking his boots and treating him like a king."

The sheriff raised a shaggy eyebrow. "That so? Folks have been fooled before. You'd be almighty s'prised how many so-called respectable people aren't what they seem. And how many who are respectable get plumb taken in."

Tim felt adrenaline surge through his body. Could this encounter with Sheriff Meade be an answer to prayer? The lawman had evidently taken the same instant dislike to Chavez that Tim had. What if Ramon Chavez wasn't all he was cracked up to be? What if even a man as shrewd and observant as Don Fernando was being fooled?

"Sheriff, can I talk to you in private?" Tim

burst out.

"Why, sure." Meade followed Tim's long stride away from the crowd to a shady spot where they couldn't be overheard. "Shoot."

"What you said about folks being taken in. I'd sure hate to see Angel Montoya shackled to someone who's not what he appears to be." Tim took a deep breath and slowly expelled it. "You've got ways of finding out things. I don't. How about you doing some nosing around concerning the senor?"

Understanding crept into Meade's eyes. "You got a personal reason fer askin'? I hear tell you packed the senorita home after her horse threw her." A knowing smile brightened the sheriff's somber features. "If I were a young feller like you, I'd be campin' on the Montoya doorstep."

Tim felt heat rush to his face before he blurted out, "A lot of good it would do with Angel's daddy bent on marrying her off to this rich hacendado — if that's what he is."

Meade's beefy hand gripped Tim's. "I've also heard tell that 'faint heart never won fair lady.' Stick that in your craw. Might be best, though, to hold off fer a spell. I'll see what I can dig up." The sheriff's keen gaze bored into Tim. "Don't fergit. This is off the record and just between us."

Relief flooded through Tim, and he pumped the sheriff's hand. The admiration he'd felt for the older man ever since childhood flared. "If there's anything to find out, you're the one to find it. Matt says you stick to a trail like a bloodhound."

"Sure, now, I wouldn't say that." But the pleased look on Meade's weatherworn face belied his words. With a final, bone-crushing squeeze of Tim's hand, he stalked away.

A few moments later, Tim saw the sheriff force his way to where Angel sat. He slipped in between her and Chavez. Tim stifled a laugh at the contrast between the thundercloud that parked on the visitor's face and the welcome in Angel's face when Meade bent over her and whispered something in her ear. She immediately rose, nodded to Chavez, and took the sheriff's arm. Heads high, they walked away from the scowling senor — and straight toward Tim.

Never thought matchmaking was part of the sheriff's duties, Tim thought, *but it sure looks like it. Meade looks like a kid with a sack full of candy.*

"Welcome again to La Casa del Sol," Angelina said when they reached Tim. She curtseyed. "Have you eaten? There is plenty of food, no matter how hungry you may be." Laughter and a softness that showed she

156

was glad he had come danced in her eyes.

Tim's rumbling stomach reminded him how long it had been since breakfast. Fine thing. He'd been so upset over his first look at Chavez he'd forgotten to eat. "Not yet." He hesitated then decided to make the most of the opportunity provided by the sheriff. "Would you care to join me?" He shot a pointed look toward Chavez, standing with crossed arms and looking daggers at them. "Or do you have other obligations?"

Angel's fingers tightened on Meade's arm. "Senor Sheriff has already requested the pleasure of my company, but I am sure he will not mind if you join us."

Meade winked at Tim. "Not at all. Haven't had the chance for a good talk with Tim in a donkey's age."

Tim bit his lip to keep from showing his amazement.

Angel's laugh rippled out. "How long is that, Senor Sheriff?"

His eyes twinkled. "A well-cared-for donkey can live for up to thirty years."

Tim's laughter died when Don Fernando spoke from behind him.

"Angelina, you are forgetting your guest." Icicles dripped from every word and left Tim speechless.

Not so Sheriff Meade. He patted Angel's

hand and drawled, "Not at all, senor. She is taking excellent care of me. In fact," he added, "Angelina has agreed to eat barbeque with me and young Sterling here. You know him, of course. Sure is lucky he found her out on the range when he did." The glare the sheriff received from his host would have withered anyone less hardy. Tim again bit his lip to keep from cackling. Doing so would *not* endear him to Don Fernando. Or remove the storm signals from the man's face. "Very well, if she has promised." The don turned and stalked off, but not until after giving his daughter a look that boded no good.

Tim turned to Angel. Her dark eyes were luminous with what he suspected were unshed tears, but she ignored the interchange and said, "Senors, shall we eat?"

The rest of the day passed in a dream for Tim. Rejoicing that he hadn't left when tempted to do so, he reveled in the time Angel sat between him and Sheriff Meade. Once, her hand brushed his when she reached for her goblet of punch. She hastily pulled it away, but twin flags of color sprang to her smooth skin. The look in her eyes when at last she pushed back from the table and said, "I must return to my other guests," left Tim walking on air.

It also emboldened him to ask, "When will I see you again?"

Every trace of the happiness that had greeted the sheriff's clever witticisms and filled the air with her delighted laughter died. "I do not know."

Tim caught Angel's furtive glance toward her father and Ramon Chavez. They stood a little distance from the merrymakers, engaged in what appeared to be an earnest conversation. No, more like an argument. Chavez gesticulated as if pleading, but Don Fernando crossed his arms and shook his head.

It reassured Tim. It appeared there would be no betrothal announcement today. Under cover of the tablecloth he found Angel's soft hand and dared to press it for a single moment. "I am praying for you," he whispered.

For a moment her fingers clung to his before pulling free. Her lips trembled. "Gracias." She rose, bestowed shaky smiles on Tim and Sheriff Meade, then raised her head as if going into battle and slowly walked away.

Tim watched her go. If he could only pack her onto Blue and spirit her away from her tyrannical father and Senor Chavez!

Sheriff Meade's voice broke into Tim's musings. He stood, hitched his belt a little higher, and touched the silver star on his vest. "I reckon I'll be moseyin' back to town. The sooner I get there, the sooner I can do some investigatin'. Timothy, my boy, you better be prayin' that I find somethin' to show 'just cause' why there shouldn't be a weddin'." The sheriff jerked a gnarled finger in Chavez's direction. "That little lady is too good for the likes of him."

A hard clasp of hands and he was gone, leaving a tiny flame of hope in Tim's soul. Sheriff Meade would turn over every rock, look behind every tree, and unearth anything suspicious in Ramon Chavez's past. If there was dishonor, the sheriff would find it and go straight to Don Fernando.

A cold chill ran down Tim's spine. Investigations took time. Even if Chavez turned out to be unworthy, would the truth be discovered soon enough to save Angel? Don Fernando had made no betrothal announcement at the fiesta, but the argument Tim had witnessed between the two men showed Chavez's impatience.

Suddenly unwilling to accept more of Don Fernando's obviously reluctant hospitality, Tim cast a fleeting glance toward Angel. She looked small. Tired. Defenseless. Tim turned away and went to find Blue.

On the way home, he called to the heavens, "God, I can't help her. You can. Protect her from evil. Unless I am badly mistaken about Chavez, if ever anyone walked through the valley of the shadow, it is Angel Montoya. Marriage with Chavez will crush the very life out of her."

By the time Tim reached the Diamond S, some of the pain in his heart had subsided. God was in control. Tim could ask for no more.

FIFTEEN

Imprisoned with invisible chains between her father and Ramon Chavez, Angelina watched Timothy Sterling mount Blue. Her heart went out to him. If only she were free to go back to him! Her fingers still tingled from the brief pressure of Tim's hand beneath the tablecloth. There had been nothing bold or daring. Just a comforting touch followed by his promise to pray for her.

When Papá moved away to speak to some guests who were preparing to leave, Angel took an involuntary step forward. Senor Chavez stopped her with a heavy hand on her arm. How different from Tim's respectful touch! Angel shook the offensive hand off under the pretense of adjusting her mantilla.

"You seem distraught, senorita. Is something troubling you?" Chavez inquired. "A quiet time with me in the courtyard away from these peones will help." He attempted to take her hand, but she backed away from him. Fear clutched at her throat. Being alone with this man in the courtyard with dusk lurking just over the horizon was the last thing she wanted.

She whipped up anger to cover her dread of such an intimate meeting. "Peones! You do my friends an injustice."

His laugh grated on her nerves. "I am surprised that a daughter of Don Fernando Montoya considers those from a lower class as friends." He stroked his bushy moustache. "Ah well, it is only for a time. After we marry, you will only associate with those of high caste."

Fury licked at her veins, but Angel kept her voice even. "We are not yet betrothed, Senor Chavez."

He waved his hands as if to dismiss her protest. "Why do you play games with me? I will settle things this night with your father. I need to get back to my hacienda in México. When I go, you shall go with me." The black eyebrows met in a scowl. "I will not stand for another such performance as you gave today. Ramon Chavez is not to be humiliated a second time."

Angel controlled a shiver and looked straight into his cruel eyes. "I did nothing to humiliate you. Sheriff Meade has known me from the time of my birth and is my friend." She emphasized the word. "As for Senor Sterling —"

"Ah, yes. Let us talk of Senor Sterling." A warning light glowed in Chavez's eyes. "Should I see him looking at you again as he did today, I will challenge this *gringo* and protect your honor."

It took all of Angel's self-control to keep from shrieking with laughter. Protect her honor? The senor sounded like a villain in a dime novel she had once read on the sly. His expression prevented an outburst. This man could be dangerous. What was to prevent him from carrying out his threat? Worse, what if Chavez hinted to her father that Tim had compromised her or made her the subject of gossip? It would strain — perhaps even shatter — the excellent relationship the Diamond S and La Casa del Sol had always enjoyed.

Excuse yourself and leave, a little voice warned. *If you do not, you will fly to Timothy's defense and confirm Chavez's suspicions. Go!*

Angel drew herself up and looked straight into her persecutor's eyes. "I am weary and must rest. *Buenas noches,* senor." She ignored his protest, raised her ruffled skirt a few inches, and walked away. But she could

164

feel his gaze boring into her back until she entered the house.

Once inside, she sagged against the heavy door then fled up the stairs to the sanctuary of her room. She bolted the door and crossed to the window seat. Heedless of possible damage to her gown, Angel curled into a ball and stared down into the courtyard. It lay empty and still except for the plaintive cry of a lone night bird. The fragrance of flowers stole through her open window, bringing a measure of relief.

One by one, highlights of the fiesta paraded through Angel's mind: The laughter and music. Sheriff Meade's kindly smile and seamed face. His whisper in her ear, inviting her to go with him to where Timothy Sterling stood a little apart from the merry crowd. The joy in Tim's face when he saw her coming, joy she knew reflected in her own. Sitting by him and making a pretense of eating while her heart thumped so loudly it seemed he must hear. The gentle touch of his hand.

"Strange," Angel told the encroaching night. "I cannot remember what we talked about. Only that he said he was praying for me." Her heart thrilled at the thought, but the interview with Chavez swept her mind clean of the more pleasant parts of the day.

Angel sat up straight, trying to remember the exact words her would-be suitor had used when he threatened Tim: *"Should I see him looking at you again as he did today, I will challenge this gringo and protect your honor."*

Angel's heart skipped. If even the arrogant Chavez saw something in Timothy Sterling's eyes that posed a threat to the betrothal, she must be right in believing that Tim cared. She felt color wash into her face, then drain away. Even if Chavez miraculously vanished, it was unlikely that Papá would ever consider Timothy Sterling worthy of his daughter's hand.

Angel crossed her arms on the windowsill and rested her head against them. Why must life be so hard? She sighed and closed her eyes. The next thing she knew, a raised voice drifted up from the courtyard below and wakened her.

"You assured me in San Francisco there would be no trouble with your daughter. Now you say I must remain here until she gets over her foolishness and agrees to a betrothal. May I remind you that Angelina is not the only suitable candidate to become my bride?" The clear air faithfully reproduced a snapping of fingers.

Angel gasped and put one hand over her mouth. She leaned closer to the window,

166

threw aside scruples, and strained to hear. Eavesdropping was not a nice thing to do, but her future was at stake.

"Do not threaten me, senor. Angelina is a dutiful daughter. She will do as I command." Papá's words fell like hailstones. "I remind you that she is very young. Not so much in years but in life itself. Twelve years studying with the nuns in the convent and living with my wife's sister and her husband have not prepared Angelina to deal with suitors."

A snort reached Angel's listening ears. "I find that hard to believe. Besides, no well-trained Spanish senorita would leave the man her father selected and choose to eat with others. When I asked her to explain herself, Angelina threw in my face that the sheriff is her friend and refused to say more. Why do you allow her to consort with gringos?"

"Consort! You forget yourself, senor." Angel thrilled to the indignation in her father's voice. "There could have been serious consequences if Senor Sterling had not found my daughter when she was hurt and brought her home. She is bound to be grateful. Let us speak no more of the matter. You will remain at La Casa del Sol until Angelina has time to accept the idea of being married."

Sadness crept into his voice. "I fear she does not wish to leave the hacienda so soon after coming home. Perhaps if you were willing to give up your holdings in México and be content here in the valley, Angelina would look more favorably on you."

After a pause, Chavez said, "I will consider it."

Angel held her breath until her father said, "The hour grows late. Let us . . ." Heavy footsteps drowned out the rest of his sentence. Once again the courtyard lay empty. This time, no bird sang.

Angel didn't move. Every trace of joy occasioned by Tim's presence at the fiesta evaporated. Her life's clock continued to tick. Although Papá had insisted on giving her some time, he hadn't budged concerning the betrothal. He expected her to go through with it, even though it meant separation. Chavez had paused before replying when her father suggested that the senor sell his hacienda and live closer to the House of the Sun. Too tired to figure out what it might mean, Angel fought back weariness and prepared for bed.

Sleep eluded her. A procession of faces and voices fought for recognition. The clock struck two. Three. Four. When a rooster announced the dawn, Angel bathed and donned the plainest gown she owned. She pulled her hair back into an unbecoming bun. Chavez had taunted Papá that she was not the only senorita available to him. Perhaps if she made herself less attractive, he would look elsewhere.

When donkeys fly. Angel groaned. Few candidates came with the dowry Chavez would receive from her father. With Angel as his wife, he would also become heir to La Casa del Sol should anything happen to Papá. She remembered the greed in Chavez's face the day he first came to the hacienda. Suspicion raced through her. What if he coveted the hacienda enough to harm Papá?

"He wouldn't. He couldn't," Angel told her mirrored image, but she couldn't shake the feeling of dread that pervaded her. When a servant tapped on the door and summoned her to breakfast, she considered sending word to her father that she was ill but curled her fingers until the nails bit into her palms. No! If Chavez really had some diabolical plan, she would discover and thwart it, starting this very day.

Although it meant risking being late to breakfast, Angel changed into a more elaborate gown. She let down her hair until it streamed to her shoulders. Then sustained by a whispered promise, *"I am praying for you,"* she swept down the staircase with all the Montoya pride instilled in her and prepared to outwit Senor Ramon Chavez.

One of Angelina Carmencita Olivera Montoya's lesser sins while at the Garcias' had been filching books from her uncle's library that she knew Tía Guadalupe would not wish her to read. Tío Miguel loved mysteries, especially those by the English author Sir Arthur Conan Doyle. Angel thoroughly enjoyed the fictional exploits of Sherlock Homes and his companion in crime solving, Dr. Watson. She studied every clue in the stories and rejoiced when she figured out the culprit's identity before the author exposed it.

Once Angel determined to play Senorita Sherlock Holmes, she abandoned attempts to avoid Ramon Chavez. On the contrary, she forced herself to spend time with him but took care to see that they were never left alone. Angel encouraged Chavez to talk about himself — even when she could barely stomach his self-importance. Little by little, she noticed flaws in his facade, small things such as slips in grammar that betrayed a lack of polish.

"If only Conchita were here to play Dr. Watson," Angel mourned. She missed her friend more with every passing day. Conchita had been a rock on which to cling. Many of the servants at the House of the Sun were much older. None had Conchita's delightful giggle. Angel had tried several young girls as a personal maid but found them unsatisfactory. Unless she had buttons she couldn't reach on the back of a frock, she seldom called for assistance.

She also missed Emilio. The new head wrangler was efficient but lacked Emilio's charm. A few letters had come. Emilio's mother was no better.

We do not know when we can return, Conchita wrote. *Emilio's familia needs us. We are happy, but I miss La Casa del Sol and you.*

Angel had never felt more alone. An unspoken truce existed between her and Papá, but she didn't know long it would last. There had been no more visits from those at the Diamond S. One day when she and her father went into Madera, Angel walked down Main Street while her father conducted business at Moore's General Store and Post Office. She halted before a modest wooden building near the far edge of town. A modest sign read CHRIST THE WAY CHURCH. Was this the church her father had mentioned all those weeks ago on the train ride? The church where he had heard someone singing about peace?

As if in answer, the words of a song floated through the open door:

"Tell me the story of Jesus,
  Write on my heart every word.
Tell me the story most precious,
  Sweetest that ever was heard."

Unwilling to enter the church, Angel tiptoed to a side window and peered inside. Timothy Sterling's sister, Ellie Stanhope — the Sierra Songbird — sang with upraised head and closed eyes. Her face wore the same expression as Tim's when he spoke of his Trailmate. Hands lightly clasped, Ellie continued:

"Tell how the angels in chorus,
  Sang as they welcomed His birth.
'Glory to God in the highest!
  Peace and good tidings to earth.'"

The beautiful voice stopped. Angel slipped away without being seen. No wonder Ellie had been the toast of San Francisco! Or that Don Carlos sought the peace his daughter now desperately needed. Would either of them ever find it?

Sixteen

"Glory to God in the highest! Peace and good tidings to earth."

The final words of the Sierra Songbird's hymn rang in Angelina's ears while she and her father climbed into the carriage for their trip back to the House of the Sun. The radiance in Ellie Stanhope's uplifted face and the assurance in her voice left no doubt; the singer believed every word. Envy filled Angel. Again she wondered whether she or her father would ever know such peace.

Her father's rich voice broke into Angelina's reflections. "I am pleased that you are becoming friends with Senor Chavez. Soon I will instruct Father Alfonso to publish the banns."

Friends? Banns? Angel felt as if she had been thrown into an icy mountain pool. Her attempts to draw out and discredit Chavez had led to this. How could she have been so foolish?

"I see no reason we cannot have the marriage fiesta by Christmas."

Horror released Angel's frozen tongue. "Oh no, Papá! I cannot possibly be ready by then." Pitting her last hope against his determination, she laid one hand on his strong arm and said, "México is far away. Once I go there, it will be a long time before I can see you again." Hot tears poured. "Are you so eager to send me away?"

"Send you away?" Papá pulled on the reins and stopped the carriage. He laughed and circled Angel with his arm. "It was to be a surprise, but since this troubles you, I will tell you the good news. Even now I am consulting with Senor Chavez. He is selling his hacienda and will remain in *los Estados Unidos,* the United States. I will keep my only daughter. He shall become the son Carmencita and I never had, your protector and la patrón of La Casa del Sol should anything happen to me."

The horrific thought dried Angel's throat. She clutched her father's hand and cried, "I do not trust him. He cares nothing for me, just for the hacienda. Please Papá, send him away!"

Her father released her and became a stranger. "You forget yourself, Angelina. Stop this childish nonsense."

Angel threw caution to the winds. "You married my mother because you loved each other. I have no love for Senor Chavez. I never will. How can you do this to me, Papá? He is a viper."

"Be still!" he thundered, whipping the horse into a gallop.

The carriage swayed. Angel had to grab for the side to keep from being thrown out. The habit of obedience she had been taught fled before the need of the moment. "If Mamá were alive she would never consent to —"

Papá glanced at her. For a split second he looked like he hated her. "I have told you to be still. No daughter of mine shall ever be allowed to speak to me as you have done. You will do as I command. The banns will be published. You will wed Senor Chavez. There will be no more rebellion."

Cowed at last, Angel shrank as far from him as possible. She had seen her father deal severely with clumsy vaqueros and lazy house servants, but never had he turned his wrath on her. Her stomach churned. It took all her willpower to keep from crying out for him to stop the carriage, that she was going to be sick.

Heavy, foreboding silence hung between them like a poisonous mist for the rest of the way home. When they arrived, her father helped Angel out of the carriage. Not a muscle of his chiseled face moved in compassion. "Remember what I said." He gave her no opportunity to reply but strode up the steps and into the house.

Angel watched him go, heartsick and at the end of her rope. Speaking of her mother had been the final attempt to reason with him. It had failed.

Two weeks later, the first of three weeks of banns for Senor Ramon Chavez and Senorita Angelina Carmencita Olivera Montoya were published.

In the days following the fiesta, Timothy Sterling raced through his range work and seized every opportunity to ride into Madera. Each trip included a visit with Sheriff Meade. At first the sheriff could find nothing to prove that although Ramon Chavez was undeniably unpleasant, he was what he claimed. Each time, Tim felt his heart sink.

After the marriage banns were published for the first time, he rode to a favorite spot, knelt beneath a sheltering oak tree, and poured his heart out in prayer. "Lord, You're the only One who can save Angel. You know I love her. Enough to stand aside if she were marrying someone worthy. Chavez is not. I feel it in every bone of my body, but Sheriff Meade hasn't been able to prove it."

Hours later, Tim mounted Blue and rode home. "I know You hear and answer every prayer," he muttered to the Lord while grooming his horse. "Sometimes it's yes. Sometimes it's no. Sometimes it's *wait.* The problem is, there's no time to wait. Time is running out."

The following week, the banns were published for the second time. Despair gnawed at Tim. "You can still step in," he told God after another sleepless night, "but You'd better hurry. There are only a few days left before the banns are published for the last time." Tim thought of what Pastor Josh had told him concerning their purpose: *"It is an opportunity for anyone who knows cause or just impediment why the two persons should not be joined can make that known."*

Tim heaved a sigh that felt as if it came from his toes. "Please, God, do something. Anything!" Gloomy and dejected, he saddled Blue for a trip to town.

He met Sheriff Meade at the edge of town, mounted on a bay and leading a saddled horse. Meade sported a grin that seemed as big as the Grand Canyon. "I got the goods on Chavez," he hollered. "*And how!* I'm ridin' out to House of the Sun now. Wanta come along and be part of the fun?"

Tim's heart leaped. "Are you serious? I wouldn't miss this for anything. What did you find out?"

"No sense chewin' my words twice," the sheriff barked. "You'll find out soon enough, boy, but I'll tell you one thing." He broke into a hoarse laugh. "What I got here is an answer to prayer. It took some doing, includin' a passel of telegrams."

Meade gestured toward the pocket of his buckskin jacket. The top of an untidy bunch of papers poked out. "If you found what's in here in a dime novel, you'd think the author was loco."

"Yee-haw!" Tim bellowed. He felt the weight of concern he'd carried on Angel's behalf disappear. "That good, huh?"

The lawman sobered. "Good for Angel, and that's what we wanted." He shut his lips in a grim line and remained silent for the rest of the way to the hacienda.

When they reached their destination and turned their horses over to a smiling vaquero, it was all Tim could do to keep from racing up the steps ahead of the sheriff. It seemed an eternity before the butler opened the front door. He looked down his nose and inquired, "Are the senors expected? I

179

am not sure if . . ."

Tim caught the steely look Sheriff Meade gave the man and wanted to laugh.

"We are not expected, but Don Fernando will see us."

The man's haughty manner wilted. "Sí. This way." He led them down the hall and out a door into the courtyard. "Senor Meade and Senor Sterling," he announced, then backed away and disappeared back into the hall.

Tim's heart went out to Angelina. Even the pink gown she wore did not lend color to her pale face. Tim smiled. He was rewarded by a faint lifting of her lips before he turned his attention to Don Fernando.

Ignoring the younger man, Montoya rose from his place beside a small table but did not offer his hand. "Sheriff, is there some way I can help you?"

"No, but I can help *you*. You, too, senorita." Meade shifted toward Chavez, who had not bothered to rise. He fumbled in his pocket and brought out a sheaf of papers. "I have here some mighty interesting reading."

Don Fernando's jaw set. "What can you have that is of any interest to us?"

"Get down off your high horse," the sheriff snapped. "Before we leave you're gonna be powerful glad we came." A slow smile spread across his face. "Bein' fond of Senorita Angel, I did some checkin' on the man who calls himself Ramon Chavez."

Chavez leaped to his feet and roared like a bull. "What do you mean? I am Ramon Chavez. I have papers to prove it!"

"That's right," Don Fernando said. "Senor Chavez's credentials are of the highest. I myself have seen them. Do you think I would be tricked when it comes to the giving of my daughter's hand?"

"You have been this time." Meade spread his papers out on the table. "You can read for yourself, but what it boils down to is this: The credentials themselves are fine, but this man ain't the right piece of fruit to dangle from the family tree. And the only haciendas he's got are in his head."

"A lie!" A hint of foam sprang to Chavez's moustache. Sweat beaded his swarthy face. He gave Tim a look of pure hatred, then spread his hands wide in appeal to Don Fernando. "The gringo cowboy is in love with your daughter. He has plotted with Senor Sheriff. You must not believe them." He struck his chest with his fist. "I am Ramon Chavez. These are my credentials. I swear by all the saints!"

"Then you'd better pray for forgiveness,"

Meade flung at him. Tim suspected it had been a long time since the sheriff had had so much fun.

Don Fernando's brows drew together. "I do not understand. If he is not Ramon Chavez, then who is he?"

"He's Ramon Chavez, all right. He's also an impostor wanted for deserting from the Mexican Army. I'm gonna take pleasure in seein' the government gets him back pronto."

Tim wanted to yell. *Thanks, God. You did something, all right, far more than I could have imagined.*

The bluster fell away from Chavez. He sank back into a chair. Angel gasped. Don Fernando paled. "How can this thing be?"

"I gotta hand it to him for comin' up with this scheme," the sheriff drawled. "He counted on pulling off a rich marriage and becoming heir to your hacienda. Maybe even knocking you off if the chance came." He ignored a muffled protest from Chavez.

"If Tim here and I hadn't suspected there was something fishy about him, he'd have succeeded." Meade's gaze bored into the cringing man. "This feller has a highly respected brother named Rodrigo. Ramon stole Rodrigo's credentials, including commendations from the Mexican government made out to *R. Chavez.* They have given him entrée into San Francisco's highest Mexican society."

Don Fernando caught his breath. "Including my sister-in-law and her husband. I shudder to think what they will say." He spun on his heel and faced Chavez. His voice turned deadly, and his eyes burned like red-hot coals. "Senor, is this true? You have accepted my hospitality and would have married my daughter under false pretenses? She was right. You are a viper!"

He raised his arm as if to strike, then slowly let if fall. A cruel smile appeared. "I could kill you myself, but there is a better way. When my vaqueros hear how you have dishonored the name of Montoya, they will hang you to the nearest oak!"

Chavez scrambled to his feet again and backed away, his face distorted. A chill went through Tim. Wicked as Chavez was, he must not be hanged. Angel would never recover from such action taking place at her beloved home. Tim took a step forward, but Sheriff Meade intervened.

"Sure now, no need for that." He locked gazes with Don Fernando. "I reckon the Mexican government can kill their own snakes."

Eyes wide with horror, Angel flew to her

father and grasped his upraised arm. "Let the sheriff take him, Papá."

The fire slowly died out of Don Fernando's face. After a long moment, he said, "Sí. La Casa del Sol must not be darkened with blood, even of one like this."

Tim relaxed. *Thanks again, Lord.*

A few moments later, Meade had Chavez tied in the saddle of the spare horse. Tim swung aboard Blue and looked up toward Angelina's window. She had not come outside with the four men. She must be relieved at her narrow escape. The scene in the courtyard had left him shaken. How much more it would have affected her!

Something white fluttered in the window. Tim touched his Stetson as if tipping it forward to shade his face from the sun. His brain buzzed. How would Chavez's treachery affect Don Fernando's attitude toward one Timothy Sterling? *Time enough to think about that later,* Tim told himself. Now he and the sheriff needed to get Chavez to town before Don Fernando reconsidered and beat the man to within an inch of his life.

"Let's go," Meade ordered. With Tim leading and Chavez sandwiched between him and the sheriff, they started down the lane that led to the road to Madera. A few moments later the sheriff mumbled, "Hold up." He turned his bay and rode back to where Don Fernando stood a little distance from the corral. Tim saw him lean forward and speak, too low for Tim or the ever-present vaqueros to hear.

"What did you tell him?" Tim burst out when the sheriff rejoined him and Chavez.

A grin split Meade's tanned face. "Not much. Just that Ramon has a wife and three *ninos* in México." He scratched his fore-head. "Didn't dare tell him before. We might not have been able to stop a necktie party . . . with Ramon here bein' the guest of honor."

Seventeen

Hidden by her bedroom draperies, Angel saw Timothy Sterling look up at her window. She snatched a handkerchief and waved it, but she kept out of sight. Tim tipped his Stetson and rode away with Ramon Chavez behind him. Sheriff Meade brought up the rear. A wave of thankfulness swept through Angel. None of the heavenly beings she had ever seen in paintings had ever looked more like an angel to her than the seasoned lawman when he exposed Chavez!

"If I hadn't been so paralyzed from the news, I would have kissed him," Angel whispered. Laughter erupted. How the men would have stared! She racked her brain, trying to remember what the sheriff had said to her father.

"He counted on pulling off a rich marriage and becoming heir to your hacienda. Maybe even knocking you off if the chance came. . . . If Tim here and I hadn't suspected there was

186

something fishy . . ."

Angel's heart pulsed with gratitude. Tim had not only been praying for her but also had obviously been "putting feet to his prayers," as she'd once heard someone say, and enlisting Sheriff Meade's help.

A groan came from the courtyard below. Angel looked down. Her father sat with shoulders slumped, his dark head buried in his hands. A low cry floated up to her. "What have I done?"

The agony in his voice cut Angel to the heart. It blotted out the bitterness she had fought for weeks. She raced out her door, down the stairs, and into the courtyard. She sped to his side and threw her arms around him. "Don't, Papá! There is no way you could have known."

He raised a ravaged face to her. "You do not understand, querida. Sheriff Meade told me more terrible news just before he left." Tears streaked his smooth face.

"What can be more terrible than what he tried to do?" she cried.

Her father tried twice before he could get the words out. "The impostor has a wife and children in México!"

Angel collapsed against him. "Then what . . . why . . . how can anyone be so wicked?"

Papá's arms tightened around her. "He has sold his soul to *el diablo.* How could I not see? I, who pride myself on knowing men. Gracias a Dios that Senor Timothy and the sheriff were wiser than I!"

Angel had never seen him so defeated or heard him sound so helpless. She stroked his hair. "Sí, Papá. But it is over now."

"It will never be over," he told her. "You shall never forgive me, and I will become the laughingstock of Madera."

A wellspring of unsuspected strength bubbled up inside Angel. Somehow she must soften this blow to her proud father. Tim's words from weeks ago flashed across her mind. *"I asked Jesus to be my Trailmate and live in my heart. . . . His presence is with me. He even taught me to forgive. . . ."*

Angel gave her father a fierce hug. "Jesús has already put it into my heart to forgive you." The moment she said the words, she knew they were true. A measure of the peace she had searched for sank deep into her soul. She continued, "Let people say what they will. Why should we care? Our true friends will understand."

Her father loosened her arms and held her out from him, a startled expression in his eyes. "When did you become so wise, querida?"

Did she dare speak what was in her heart? Angel hesitated and groped for just the right words. "Senor Timothy — the day we went riding with Sarah and Conchita. He said that after he asked Jesús to be his Trailmate and live in his heart, he was never alone. Jesús' presence was always with him. It taught him to forgive."

His mouth fell open. Blank astonishment filled his face. Then he burst out, "Would to God I could experience that!"

Angel felt they stood at a crossroads. She opened her mouth, and words came of their own volition. "Papá, when Senor Timothy is troubled, he does not confess to a priest. He goes straight to his heavenly Father. He said that God is the only One who holds forgiveness and offers help."

Something flickered in his eyes. Was it a spark of hope? "What else did Senor Timothy say?"

Angel steadied her voice. "That no problem is too big for Him, but we have to ask. He said that in the holy Bible Jesús promised His followers that if they would ask and seek and knock they would receive and find, and ways would be opened to them."

Papá looked as if he had seen a ghost. His voice hoarsened. "If only it could be true!" He shook his head. "How can it be that simple? Angelina, how did Senor Timothy look when he told you these things?"

She closed her eyes, remembering. "His face glowed like the morning sun."

"Like Senor Fallon's face on the day he came and said God loves me and offers me hope." Papá passed a shaking hand over his eyes. "I have not been able to get it out of my mind. Or the words of peace the Sierra Songbird sang that day when I was passing the church. I would sell my soul to possess it!"

So would I. But Angel did not destroy the fragile moment by expressing her own needs. "Have you seen Senor Fallon since that time? Perhaps if you talked with him —"

"I have been too proud." Her father's confession hung in the still air.

"And now?" Angel held her breath, feeling once again they stood at a crossroads.

"I am a broken man, Angelina. I can no longer hold my head high." He gently put her from him and rose. His lips twisted in a wry smile. "To think Don Fernando Montoya would come to this — forced to seek out a former bandido for help. But I cannot go on living without peace."

Words sprang to Angel's mind. "It is not the bandido who will bring peace, Papá, but the message he carries. The same message about which Senora Ellie Stanhope sings. The day we went to Madera, I heard her singing of peace and good tidings to earth. I peeped into the window of Christ the Way Church. The senora's expression showed she believed every word." Angel laid one hand over her heart. "I would give all I possess to have the peace that she and Senors Timothy and Fallon have."

Only the splash of water in the fountain broke the silence that followed. At last Papá said in a tone so low that she had to lean forward to hear him, "Then, my Angelina, we shall ask and seek and knock. It may be my last hope — and yours."

Through tear-blinded eyes Angel watched her father leave the courtyard. She had never loved him more.

The next morning Papá summoned Angelina to his study before breakfast. His lined face showed he had slept no better than she had. All night Angel had tossed and turned, wondering what would come of their visit to the man who had flashed in and out of her father's life and made such a lasting impression.

Did not Timothy Sterling touch your heart-strings during your first real conversation with him? an inner voice demanded. *If Dios has something more for you and your papá to know, who can say what means He will use? Sheriff Meade told your father to get down off his high horse. Perhaps Dios in His wisdom saw that Don Fernando needed to be humbled in order to be taught.*

"All I know is that You heard and answered my prayer to be saved from Senor Chavez. I had given up hope," Angel whispered. She blinked back tears. Each time she thought of the interview with Sheriff Meade and his unmasking of Chavez, she pinched herself to make sure she really had been spared from the impostor's wicked schemes.

"I can wait no longer," Papá announced in a somber voice. "I tremble to think of what may happen when we talk with Senor Fallon, but we shall go to him today." He shrugged his shoulders. "*Qué será, será.* If he still wears peace in his countenance, we must learn his secret and that of others. At times I have even thought of seeking out Pastor Stanhope. He also wears peace like a banner." The don's mouth set in a grim line. "I could not go. Can you imagine what Father Alfonso would say?"

Angel remembered the lack of under-standing the priest had shown when she went to him for help. "I — I don't want to think about it."

"Nor do I." He gave her a twisted smile. "But after what has happened, I feel compelled to take steps that until now I would never have considered. First we have our morning meal; then we go."

"Do you know where Senor Fallon lives?" Angel inquired.

Papá raised one eyebrow. A twinkle flashed into his dark eyes and drove away his sober expression. "Sí. I know all that goes on in Madera and in the valley." He laughed. "How else can your papá rule La Casa del Sol? Make haste, querida. I wish to leave within the hour." He hesitated, and a cloud swept across his face. "Let us speak no more of this until we break the fast and are on our way."

"Yes, Papá."

But it was all Angel could do to refrain from speculating on the outcome of their visit and to choke down a few bites of breakfast. On the way to the Fallon home, doubts assailed her. Could a former bandido truly offer anything to erase the worry lines in her father's face? Heal the turmoil in his heart and blot out the torment in his dark eyes?

Please, God. . . . Angel could not continue. Once more she felt that she and her father stood at a crossroads, a crossroads that had no sign pointing the way they should go.

Torn between hope and fear, Angelina rode on Blanca without talking. Now and then she stole a look at her father's set face. A wave of love for him filled her. Unlike the way he usually rode, straight-backed and head held high, Papá slumped in the saddle and silently stared ahead. Not until they reached the Fallon home did he rouse from wherever his thoughts had been and help her swing down from the saddle.

The walk from the hitching rail in front of the Fallons' modest dwelling to the front porch looked miles long to Angelina. If she and Papá found what they were looking for inside the humble, vine-covered cottage, would it open a chasm between them and those who inhabited the House of the Sun? Would it separate her from Conchita even more than the long miles that now stretched between them?

Angel shuddered at the thought. She half turned, unwilling to risk it. Then a glance at her father's haggard face sent a fierce wave of protectiveness through her. She must do whatever it took to bring peace to his soul — *and to yours,* a little voice reminded.

He raised a gloved hand and knocked on the frame of the screen door, which permitted a view of a simple but homey room. When a lovely, dark-haired woman came to the door, he removed his sombrero and asked, "Is Senor Fallon home?"

A tall man stepped up behind her. Silver streaked his red hair. But the joy in his face when he gently put the woman aside and flung wide the screen door clogged Angelina's throat with tears.

"Don Fernando, I have waited a long time for you," Fallon cried, extending a timeworn hand. "Come in, please. This is my wife, Abby. We have two boys, but they are off visiting friends."

No fine paintings or tapestries hung on the plain white walls of the main room, but Abby Fallon's welcoming smile went straight to Angel's heart. "You must be Angelina. Welcome to our home." She made no apology for the contrast between it and La Casa del Sol. She needed none. Although lacking in elegance, the room had been furnished with love, the same love that glowed from Abby's beautiful eyes when she looked at her husband.

Once seated, her father came straight to the point. "Senor Fallon, what must I do to have the peace of God in my life? I have lighted candles, kept the fast and feast days, given of my wealth, confessed to Father Alfonso, and done penance for my sins. Peace has not come. What more can I do?"

His despairing cry and the look in his face cut Angel to the heart. She clasped her hands until her knuckles whitened and waited for the former bandido's reply.

EIGHTEEN

A little pool of silence fell over the Fallon home. Then Angel's father asked again in the hoarse voice so different from his usual tone, "What must I do to have peace?"

Angelina sat as if turned to stone, her gaze riveted on Red Fallon's seamed face. The compassion in his eyes and kindness in his face helped to still the hard beating of her heart. She felt as if she stood on the brink of a great discovery, one that could change both Papá's life and her own forever.

Red picked up a worn, black-covered book from a nearby table and stroked it with callused fingers. "Senor Montoya, my favorite person in the holy Bible other than God and Jesus is a not Peter, or Paul, or any of those you call saints."

Angel felt a rush of disappointment. She sent a quick look at her father and saw her feelings reflected in his eyes. Was it for this that they had made the long ride from La

Casa del Sol?

Fallon let the pages of the book fall open. "My favorite person is a man much like yourself: highly respected with a position to maintain. His name means 'victor of the people.' Two thousand years ago, Nicodemus, who after the crucifixion helped prepare Jesus's body for burial, came to Jesus by night."

A smile lit up Red's craggy face. "Some call Nicodemus a coward for coming during the darkness. I think perhaps he could not get through the crowds around the Master in the daytime."

Angel leaned forward in her chair. What would this remarkable man say next?

Fallon's voice lowered. An indescribable look brightened his face. "Nicodemus was a member of the Sanhedrin, the highest and most powerful religious and political body within Judaism. He knew the teachings of the Law. Why would such a man seek out a lowly carpenter from Nazareth?"

For the same reason my father and I came to you, a former bandido. My father saw in you something we desperately need. Angel trembled at the thought.

Red confirmed it. "Nicodemus must have realized he needed something more. He called Jesus 'Rabbi' and said He was a teacher come from God, for no man could perform miracles unless God was with him."

Papá had not moved a muscle during Fallon's story. "I still do not understand why you admire this Nicodemus so much."

Abby Fallon spoke for the first time. Her eyes sparkled, and her voice rang with joy. "Not for what he was, senor, but because his coming to Jesus provided the setting for the most important teaching of all time. John 3:16 tells us 'For God so loved the world, that he gave his only begotten Son, that whosoever believeth in him should not perish, but have everlasting life.' "

Her father's hands spread wide in a gesture of protest. "I already believe Jesús is the Son of God. I have kept the laws of my church since childhood, yet I have no peace such as I see in your faces and heard in the Sierra Songbird's voice. My daughter feels the same. Senor Timothy Sterling spoke to her of finding peace when he invited Jesús to become his Trailmate and ride with him. Angelina saw that same peace in his face. Why does it elude us? And if Dios loves us, why did He let my Carmencita and our little son die?"

A lump of misery sprang to Angel's throat. How could anyone answer that? But a flash of insight told her it must be answered if

199

her father was ever to find peace.

Sadness replaced the joy in Abby's face. "I, too, have asked that question," she confessed. "When those we love are taken, often without warning, it is hard to accept. I sometimes think our great losses help us to catch a glimpse of how God felt when He saw His Son crucified by the very ones He came to save. There is hope, though. The psalmist David tells us that weeping may endure for a night, but joy comes in the morning. If we hope and trust in the Lord, we shall see our loved ones again."

"Yes." Red turned pages of his Bible. "We also have God's promises. I was amazed to learn there are more than a hundred verses that command us to trust in the Lord and as many commanding us to fear not. The apostle Paul wrote to the Philippians, 'And the peace of God, which passeth all understanding, shall keep your hearts and minds through Christ Jesus.'"

Papá leaped to his feet. "I would give all I own to possess that peace!"

Red also stood. "All your lands and buildings and cattle are not enough to purchase it. We cannot earn it, no matter what we do or how hard we try. Salvation is a free gift from our heavenly Father, bought and paid for on the cross at Calvary. Peace is a result.

All that is required of us is to humble ourselves and accept His gift."

Angel held her breath until it came out in a little *whoosh*. Could Papá ever acknowledge the truth that had flown into her heart like a bolt of lightning and illumined her soul? If he did, one of the barriers between her and Timothy Sterling would be broken. If not . . . She pushed the thought aside.

Her father sighed. "I have always honored the *padres* who brought religion to this land. They suffered great hardship. Are you saying everything they taught is wrong?"

"Oh no, Senor Montoya," Red protested. He laid a heavy hand on the don's shoulder. "Those early followers of God did great good. What I discovered is something more: the need to make Jesus my personal Savior. Months ago I came to you. Like those padres, I traveled long miles to carry a message of hope." He stopped and looked directly into his guest's face. "My prayer is that you will do whatever you must to find peace."

Words rushed out of Angel's mouth before she could control them. "Senor Fallon, I do not mean to be ill-mannered, but how can you know?" She searched for the right words. "You do not appear to be a learned man, yet you speak wisely."

The most humble expression she had ever seen appeared. Then Red said, "I have two teachers, Senorita Angel." He smiled at Abby. "The first is my wife. After I invited Jesus into my heart and became a new man, she saw beyond my sinful past and helped me to learn what I should have learned long before."

"And the second teacher?"

Red clasped his Bible in both hands and laid it over his heart. "The Holy Spirit. When you ask, that Spirit will lead you into all truth."

Joy flooded Angel. *As it has led me this day. Jesús, please show Papá as well.*

"Will you not think on these things, Senor Montoya?" Red pleaded.

Papá's usual composure returned. "What have I to lose? I have tried everything else and failed." He did not wait for a reply. "Come, Angelina. The hours have flown. We must be on our way."

Abby intervened. "Not before you share a meal with us."

To Angel's delight, her father smiled and became the charming hacendado once more. "We shall be happy to do so if we are not imposing."

"Not at all." Red grinned and patted his stomach. "The only danger is in making a pig of yourself!"

Angel gasped at his daring but relaxed when her father just laughed.

She hadn't known how hungry she was until the four of them sat around a small table at one end of the large room. A spotless red-and-white-checked cloth held matching napkins, plain china dinnerware, and a small bouquet of wildflowers. Again Angel marveled at Abby's lack of apology. The hostess served beans flavored with bacon, bread warm from her oven, and butter she said she had churned that morning as if they were the finest filet mignon or lobster. Angel ate until she was ashamed of herself, then reluctantly turned down a second piece of apple pie.

Papá did not. He finished every crumb before telling Abby, "If you ever need a job, I will make a place for you at La Casa del Sol."

Abby turned pink but only said, "Thank you, senor, but my place is here with my husband and boys."

The look she exchanged with her husband reminded Angel of Conchita's expression when she rode away in the carriage with Emilio. Angel looked around the humble dwelling. If a certain tall cowboy from the Diamond S made a home for her like this, could she be happy? *Sí,* her heart whispered. She felt a blush rise from the collar of her blouse and ducked her head to hide her burning face.

A short time later, Papá helped Angel aboard Blanca and prepared to mount his own horse for the long ride home.

Red Fallon held out a gnarled hand. "You will come again." Not a question. A statement of belief.

"Sí." A final grip and her father prepared to mount. "You have given me much to think of this day."

"That's good." Red paused. "Senor Montoya, you have said you will do anything to find peace." He held out his worn Bible. "Take this book. Read what those who were closest to Jesus had to say. Even though you may already know much of what it contains, I ask you to read as if you had never heard it before. Also read the words I have written beside some of the verses."

Papá hesitated. "Will you not need it?"

"My wife has a Bible we can use." Red's face glowed. "Besides, many of the words are written in my heart."

The don silently took the Bible and placed it in his saddlebag. He mounted his horse and called, "Gracias. I shall return it to you some day."

"There is no hurry. God go with you."

The riders started back toward the House of the Sun. Angel's heart beat high with hope, and she urged Blanca into a ground-covering lope. But at the top of a slight rise above the Fallon home, she slowed and looked back. Abby Fallon's dark head just reached the heart of the tall man with the silver-streaked hair. His arm lay across her shoulders. "They have little, but they are happy," she murmured.

Her father, who had also paused, nodded. "Any man who is blessed with the love of a good woman has no reason not to be happy. Come, querida. We must go home."

Neither spoke again for a few miles; then Angel gathered her courage and asked, "Papá, do you believe what Senor Fallon said?"

He did not answer for a long time. At last he spoke. "How can one not believe when a man is so sincere and wears a smile like an angel? However, there is much to consider. I fear Father Alfonso will not approve. Still, I know I must do what is right." His keen gaze bored into hers. "What of you?"

"I have already asked Jesús to live in my heart and felt the peace Senor Fallon's Bible says passes understanding." Angel raised a gloved hand from the reins and let it fall. "I cannot explain, but it is here, and I feel free." She pressed her hand to her chest. "If only you can find it, Papá!"

"I shall try." He fell silent, but Angel's heart kept time with her horse's flying feet. When they reached home, Angel bade her father good night and wearily climbed the stairs. Exhausted by a multitude of emotions and the long ride, she fell asleep moments after her head hit the pillow . . . but not before hugging to herself the new joy that had entered her life.

Angel's joy was short-lived. The next morning, Father Alfonso knocked at the door of La Casa del Sol just as she came to the top of the stairs. Dressed for riding and exulting in the early dawn, dread filled her when the butler opened the door and she heard the priest say, "I must see Senor Montoya. It is urgent."

Angel gathered her long skirts about her and stepped back out of sight. What was so urgent as to bring Father Alfonso at this hour? Had he learned of their visit to the Fallons and come to chastise them? If not that, what? With a quick prayer she pushed aside the thought of breakfast and went back to her room, fearing the summons she knew would come but not knowing why.

NINETEEN

Angelina curled up on the window seat of her bedroom and gazed down on the sunlit courtyard. The fragrance of flowers damp from their daily watering stole up to the open window. Their scent failed to banish the feeling that Father Alfonso's early morning call meant trouble. "Why did he have to come now, when I was so happy and Papá had promised to consider Senor Fallon's words?" Angel murmured.

A small cloud scooted over one edge of the sun and dimmed the brilliant morning. Angel shivered. Too often a lone cloud heralded the arrival of others that grumbled thunder over the valley. Angel felt the joy she had experienced the night before when she invited Jesús into her heart begin to pale, crowded out by unreasonable fear. All the telling herself Father Alfonso's visit might not have anything to do with her was in vain. Something deep inside warned it had everything to do with her.

Angel sat bolt upright. The priest had been upset with her for questioning a father's authority. What if he had come to plead with her father to send her to a convent? She leaped from the window seat. "Papá would never agree. He knows I could not live behind cloistered walls. Besides, he would not send me away unless I was married."

Angel froze. Could the reason for Father Alfonso's visit be that Senor Chavez had escaped from Sheriff Meade and returned to make trouble? Terror gripped her. She wanted to rush down the stairs and into her father's office. To learn for herself what had caused the priest to come to La Casa del Sol at this time of day.

She started for the door and thought better of it. "Papá would not approve of my interrupting him when the priest is here."

Angel returned to her window seat. The innocent-looking cloud had grown until it blocked the sun's rays. The earth lay still and shadowed, unbroken by a single bird-song. Even the distant sound of vaqueros at work seemed muted — as if the world waited for it knew not what, just as she did.

At last, a servant tapped at Angel's door. "Senor Montoya wishes to see you."

She waited until the sound of his footsteps died, then sent a quick prayer toward heaven. "Jesús, You promised never to leave me. Please help me now." Her feet dragged on the way downstairs, and the hall had never looked so long or forbidding. Angel's heart thudded. What would she find when she entered her father's office?

There was no sign of Father Alfonso, but her father stood in the open doorway. Angel had not seen him wear such a joyous expression since well before the sheriff and Timothy Sterling had taken Ramon Chavez away. Now he embraced her and said, "Come in, querida. I have wonderful news."

Relief that her imaginings had evidently been wrong left Angel feeling weak. She sagged against her father. How foolish she had been to attach so much significance to an early morning call by the priest! Papá's face would never glow with happiness if anything was amiss.

He gazed at her and rested his hands on one knee. "Father Alfonso has received word that his godson is coming to visit. He is only a few years older than you, Angelina. Senor Menendez is a handsome young man who has recently fallen heir to a large hacienda near Fresno.

"Father Alfonso has told him about you,

209

and he is eager to become betrothed." A reverent look came into his eyes. "His name is Teodoro, which means a gift from God. This is more than I deserve after not listening to you concerning Senor Chavez!"

Angel felt herself grow cold, as if life itself were draining out of her. Her throat burned with anger and unshed tears. She wanted to cry out, to tell her father that unless she married Timothy Sterling she would never marry at all. But if her life had depended on it, not a single word could have broken through her constricted throat.

Some of Papá's excitement faded. "Have you nothing to say about this most wonderful news? Think, Angelina. When you go to the house of your husband, you shall not be far away from your papá." He rubbed his hands together, obviously well pleased with this latest turn of events.

Angel had to say something. Anything that would give her an opportunity to escape. "It — it is all so sudden." She faltered. "When does Senor Menendez come?"

"Ah, that is the best news of all. He arrives *mañana.*" Her father stood. "Now there is much to do. This afternoon I will consult further with Father Alfonso." He patted her shoulder then strode to the door. "This day has the sun truly shone on La

Casa del Sol." He walked out of the office and down the hall, whistling as he went.

The sound of her father's footsteps beat into Angel's brain like a hammer on an anvil. When they died away, she fled to her room as she had done many times before. By the time she reached it, she had relived every moment in the office. She covered her mouth to keep from screaming. The new suitor a gift from Dios? Never!

When Angel regained control, she declared, "Senor Menendez may be all that Father Alfonso said he is and more, but it makes no difference." She staggered to her window seat and noticed the sky had grown as dismal as she felt. "I shall never marry him. Even if it means Papá casts me aside forever." The thought brought pain so sharp Angel marveled that it did not kill her, but it failed to weaken her determination.

Fine words, the persistent little voice that often taunted her said, *but just how do you propose to escape?*

Angel gave a final glance out the window. "Papá said he would go see Father Alfonso this afternoon. When he does, I shall ride away from La Casa del Sol. Perhaps forever."

Where will you go?

Angel closed her eyes. She thought of the

211

love in Timothy Sterling's face when he looked at her, and her heart beat faster. "I will go to the one I love."

Somehow Angel lived through the midday meal, smiling much and saying little while her father exulted over their good fortune in the person of Teodoro Menendez. But the moment the siesta hour arrived and she saw her father leave, Angel stole out, rounded up Blanca, and headed for the Diamond S. She pushed her horse to the limit. Both were hot and breathless when they reached their destination.

Angel had been so engrossed in successfully getting away she hadn't planned what to do when she arrived at the ranch. Somehow she must see Timothy alone. See him and enlist his help in the daring plan that had come to her as she rode. To her dismay the place looked deserted when she arrived. "What should I do?" she prayed.

Trust Me.

Had someone spoken? Angel shook her head. The voice had come from deep inside, but it was unlike anything she had ever heard. She slowly walked up the steps, crossed the spacious front porch, and knocked on the door. No one came.

A moment later the sound of rapid hoof-beats came from behind her, and a familiar

212

voice said, "Angel? What are you doing here? Everyone's gone but me. I saw you flying along like white lightning, but you were too far away to hear me when I called."

She whirled as Timothy Sterling reined in Blue and slid to the ground. "I ran away."

"Again?" His eyebrows quirked.

"Sí." Desperation overcame modesty and long years of tradition. "Senor Timothy, do you wish to marry me?"

Tim's mouth fell open, but there was no mistaking his love when he quietly said, "More than you can imagine. Angel, what has happened to bring you here like this?"

She ran to him and threw herself into his arms. "Father Alfonso's godson is coming mañana, and Papá rejoices. How can I marry Teodoro Menendez when I" — she gulped — "when I love another man?"

Tim's strong arms tightened around her. "Angelina, am I the man you love?"

"From the moment I awakened and saw you under the oak tree." Angel hid her face against his vest then looked up. "I do not understand. Yesterday at the home of Senor Fallon I asked Jesús to live in my heart. Why did He let this happen?"

Tim looked stupefied. "You asked Jesus into your heart?"

"Sí. And Papá promised to think on all

213

that Senor Fallon and his wife told us." Angel drew in a quivering breath and hopelessness attacked again. "Last night I was happy. This morning Father Alfonso came."

Tim's voice turned to steel. "Don Fernando is bent on arranging the marriage?"

Angel straightened and fired her one and only shot. Her voice sounded thin in her ears when she said, "The only way I can be saved is if I am already wed to another man. Take me away. Now. We will find someone to marry us. Once I am your wife, there will be nothing Papá or Father Alfonso can do about it."

Tim caught her close and held her as if unwilling to ever let her go. "It is all I have dreamed of since I found you lying helpless beneath the oak. My family warned me it could never be, but I told them that if God willed it, it would happen."

Greater love than Angel had ever known, even when her father held her tight, surrounded her. She felt as if she had come home.

A heartbeat later Tim gave a great sigh, released her, and stepped back. She sensed what was coming before he spoke.

"I would give all I own to elope with you," he said in a ragged voice. "The temptation is terrible." He swallowed hard. "I can't do it, Angel. What kind of life would we have should we begin it by breaking God's commandment to 'honor thy father and thy mother'? Eloping would dishonor Don Fernando even more than the business with Ramon Chavez. It would also break his heart. Even if he didn't have the marriage annulled and sometime forgave us, he might never forgive God for letting it happen."

Tim's words fell like harsh pebbles pelting Angel's heart. "Then I am condemned to a life of misery."

"No!" Tim squared his shoulders and gathered her close. "I will do the honorable thing and take you home. I shall face Don Fernando like a man and ask permission to call on you. I will tell him I love you the way he loved your mother. Surely that will soften his heart." Tim paused then whispered, "This is to seal my promise."

His lips met hers in a brief kiss, and then once more he thrust her from him. Angel knew she would never forget the look of relinquishment in his eyes. He helped her mount Blanca, leaped astride Blue, and turned toward La Casa del Sol, the house where sunlight no longer dwelt for Angel.

Lost in misery and fearing what lay ahead, she paid little attention to her surroundings

215

except to notice that the sky was growing dark although the hour was not late. They rounded a bend in the road. Tim halted Blue and grabbed Blanca's reins. She skidded to a stop, bringing Angel out of her trance-like state. Angel stared ahead and gasped.

Three masked riders blocked their way, two on horseback and one standing beside a third horse.

"What — ?" Tim vaulted from the saddle and confronted them. "Who are you, and what do you want?"

The one on foot gave an evil laugh. "We heard about the senorita ridin' out alone and meetin' you. Bein' smart hombres, we s'spected she'd do it again. Couldn't catch up with her and that white horse of her'n on the way to the Diamond S but figgered you'd be bringin' her home. Or somewheres else." His voice dripped innuendo, and the other two snickered.

"We aim to take the little lady and git a pretty penny out of her daddy. Move out of the way, sonny."

Tim's face blazed. "Why you . . ." He leaped forward but too late. One of the riders sent his horse crashing into Tim and knocked him off balance. Before he could steady himself, the man on the ground

216

sprang forward, swung the butt of a pistol against Tim's head, and kicked him in the ribs. He fell without a sound.

Rage released Angel from her horror but not soon enough. She heard Blue whinny and race off. Blanca turned away from the man with the pistol, but he caught her bridle and forced her to stand still. He hauled Angel off the horse as a second man leaped to the ground and snatched Tim's bandanna from his neck. He took a small bottle from his pocket and poured the contents over the kerchief.

"Here, Boss, this'll keep her quiet."

The boss grabbed the bandanna and shoved it over Angel's nose and mouth. She became aware of a slightly sweet odor that made it hard to breathe. She struggled to be free but felt herself weakening. Then, darkness.

TWENTY

Timothy Sterling awoke to a growl of thunder. He raised one hand to his throbbing head and discovered a baseball-sized knot where his Stetson should have been. He tried to sit up then wished he hadn't. Dizzy and disoriented, he took three tries to get to his feet. He must have been attacked. But why and by whom?

Something nudged Tim's arm. He turned. Blue's second nudge helped to clear Tim's mind. "Angel?" His only answer was a boom of thunder and a flare of lightning that lit up the gray sky. Sneering words taunted: *"We aim to take the little lady and git a pretty penny out of her daddy."*

Sick with horror, every detail of the encounter flashed into Tim's mind. Guilt ate into him like a dose of acid. "Angel came to me for protection, Lord. A lot of good I did her! How long was I knocked out, anyway?"

He reached for the revolver he always carried. The holster was empty. Now what? Even if he could find Angel, what could he do against three outlaws? Well, he had to try. And he still had his rifle in its scabbard. "Why didn't they take you, Blue? How'd you get away? Anyway, thanks for coming back."

Blue nickered and rubbed his soft nose against his master's shoulder. Tim stuck his foot in the stirrup, swung into the saddle, and sat still until he regained his balance. Why should mounting Blue leave him reeling? The day had cooled, and he reached to button his vest. His fingers stilled. "Where's my neckerchief? I'd hate to lose it, especially after it came back with those infernal coins from Don Fernando."

Satisfaction for the way Matt had handled the haughty senor tilted Tim's lips up but only for a second. No time for gloating. He scowled and guided Blue to a slight knoll nearby. Eyes made keen from long years of range observation did a 360-degree examination of the landscape. In spite of the growing gloom, Tim detected a dust cloud some distance ahead and off to the west. His heart thumped. "Well, Lord, it may not be them, but it's the only clue we have."

Tim touched his still-aching head.

"Should I ride back to the Diamond S? Or La Casa del Sol?" Something wet spattered on his bare head. He glared at the sky. "Great. It hasn't rained for weeks. Why now? By the time I can get help, what tracks those riders leave will be washed out." He grimaced. "Sorry, Lord. You know where they took Angel. You can help me find her."

A quick touch of his heels and Blue leaped forward toward the west. The dust cloud soon disappeared in the soft but steady rain that came, but Tim kept Blue headed straight for where he had seen it. His mind ran like a caged squirrel. As usual, he talked to his horse, the best listener he had outside of his Trailmate. "Rain and dust mean mud, Old Boy. If it doesn't get any worse than this, we can probably find some tracks. Of course if it pours, they'll be washed out."

Blue turned his head and whinnied. Tim patted his neck and went on sifting ideas. "On the other hand, those galoots didn't look like they'd take kindly to riding in the rain. I'll bet a dollar to a jackrabbit they'll be looking for a place to hole up." Excitement spurted. "There's that old, deserted homesteader's cabin in a draw a few miles from here. Same direction we're heading. What do you say we mosey over there and see what we find?" Damp but determined,

Tim urged Blue into a gallop and added, "Okay, Lord, let's go find Angel."

Tim knew from long experience that distances in this part of California were tricky. He tried to calculate where he'd seen the dust cloud but took no chances. Long before he reached the spot, he slowed Blue and began watching the trail. At last his sharp gaze found what he sought: two clear sets of hoofprints in a rain-softened patch of earth. Tim jumped from the saddle and examined them. His blood raced. He'd know those prints if he saw them again.

A little later he found more. They differed from the first ones. A cowboy yell started at his toes, but Tim squelched it before it could burst from his throat. He wanted to urge Blue into a dead run but discarded the idea. "We gotta play it smart," he told the roan. "If those dirty skunks have any brains at all, they may leave a rear guard. Or could be they don't know I'm following. Probably figured that blow to my noggin would put me out of commission. Maybe permanently."

He rubbed the aching knot. "I still can't figure out what happened to my Stetson. A knock on the head hard enough to raise this goose egg coulda killed me if I hadn't been wearing my hat. The guys would naturally take my revolver, but who'd want my hat and kerchief? And why?"

Tim puzzled over it for a time, then muttered, "Trouble is, Lord, those riders can't be purely dumb or they couldn't have pulled this off so slick." Ice water spread through Tim's veins. "How could they know Angel would be riding alone today? She didn't plan on it. They must have been watching her and hoping for a chance. Or someone at the House of the Sun was keeping them informed."

He snorted. "Not likely. Everyone there sings the praises of 'the blessed senorita.' Besides, it's common knowledge that Don Fernando would horsewhip, maybe even kill, any vaquero who dared spy on his daughter."

When daylight began to fade and Tim could no longer see the few tracks not wiped out by the rain, he doggedly kept going toward the cabin. He rejoiced over his long years in the saddle. He had ridden over every inch of the Diamond S. He knew it well enough to find his way to the cabin in pitch dark. Yet when a few stars poked holes through the murky night Tim thanked God for them.

One good thing. Since there had been

nothing familiar about the masked riders, they might not know the area as well as their pursuer did. "Can't count on it, though," Tim groused. "Especially if they know about the cabin."

His first whiff of woodsmoke made him even more cautious. Tim halted Blue a little way from their destination. He shouldered his rifle and silently stole toward the cabin, careful not to brush against bushes that would betray his presence to the men inside or the four horses tied to a tree a little way off. Blanca's white coat was the most welcome sight Tim had seen in hours.

The cabin tilted crazily to one side. This gave Tim a definite spying advantage. He eased his way to a glassless window whose rag of a curtain tilted enough for him to peer in. He stifled a cry of joy. Three men huddled around a rude table that held several bottles. The smell of whiskey reached Tim's nostrils. From the sound of the maudlin voices and cursing, the men had been drinking for some time. Tim strained to see their faces in the shadowy room lighted only by a single candle. Nothing.

Should he thrust his rifle inside the window and order the men to throw down their weapons? No. Too chancy. Men desperate to save their hides couldn't be counted on to act reasonably. There had to be a better way. Tim's gaze traveled to a partially open door at the far side of the squalid room. The room at the back also had a window. It could prove a less dangerous way to rescue Angel. But first he must wait until the kidnappers slept.

After what felt like an eternity, the men staggered to bedrolls laid out on the filthy floor. Still Tim waited. He must be positive that all three were in a drunken stupor before he made his move.

"Lord, I'll only have one chance," he whispered. "I'm sure gonna need Your help." He counted to one hundred and then sneaked around behind the cabin and pushed aside the tattered window curtain. His heart ached when he saw in the dim light from the other room a curled-up figure lying on a broken cot a few feet from the window. There must be a spark of manhood in at least one of Angel's captors, enough to keep the prisoner from sleeping on the floor.

Not daring to speak for fear of rousing the men, Tim slipped his rifle inside the window and gently prodded Angel's shoulder.

She didn't move.

He tried again.

She lay as if dead.

Tim's mouth dried. Surely they wouldn't have killed her! He stuck his head in the window and sniffed. Chloroform! She might not rouse for hours.

Great drops of sweat dampened Tim's forehead. Waiting to see if it would wear off was out of the question. He had to get her away. Now, while her captors slept. With a frantic plea for help, he forced head and shoulders through the window frame. Thank God for the man who had made the windows larger than those found in the usual homesteader's cabins! Tim pulled the rest of his body through and dropped inside the small space between the wall and the cot. He picked up Angel's inert form.

The cot creaked.

The snoring in the other room ceased — and stopped Tim in his tracks. He held his breath until it felt like his head might explode. *Dear God, please don't make me use the rifle. I don't dare try to close the door.*

What seemed like a lifetime later, the snoring resumed. Tim lifted Angel through the window and carefully lowered her to the ground. He climbed out, snatched her up, and crept away with her in his arms. Hating to leave her for even a second, he set his jaw and laid her down behind a clump of bushes. "We aren't through here, Lord," he mumbled. Step by cautious step Tim made his way to where the horses were tied. "Lord, You opened the mouths of the dumb. Begging your pardon, but it would sure help if You'd keep these critters' mouths shut right now."

He freed Blanca. The kidnappers' cayuses could never outrun Blue or Blanca. She made no sound, and Tim silently thanked God. He led her to where he'd left Blue. Next, he carried Angelina to the horses and mounted Blanca with the girl in his arms. Blue would follow. Only one task remained, risky, but necessary. Tim turned the white mare back to the kidnappers' horses. A quick slash of reins, a slap on the rump, and the horses melted into the night.

So did Tim and Angel.

Early the next morning, Tim rode up to the Diamond S. Angel still lay unconscious in his arms. Blue trailed behind them. Tim's head had pounded so hard during the last endless mile home that if not for God-given strength he wouldn't have made it. Now his relief was so great he swayed in the saddle.

Matt Sterling bolted down the steps from the porch. "What has happened?" He reached Tim. "Angelina! Dear God, is she dead?"

Tim handed her to Matt. "No. Drugged." He lurched from the saddle. Regret and shame washed over him. "Take good care of her. I couldn't." He watched Matt stride away, wishing he had the energy to follow. What did it matter? "Tired. So tired." Tim sank to the ground. "Somebody take care of the horses." His head spun. His mouth felt dryer than cotton in August. He tried to get up, but it wasn't worth the effort. Solita and Sarah would care for Angel. "Water." It came out as a croak.

Strong arms lifted him. Ice-cold water poured into his mouth. "Not too much," a familiar voice warned.

"Seth?" His brother had never looked better to Tim's weary eyes. But why were there two of him?

"Yes. Don't try to talk. We have to send word to Don Fernando that Angel has been found. He is out of his mind with worry."

"Tell him —" Words failed. Not until after Seth picked him up and carried him into the house could Tim finish the sentence, and then only in his mind: *Tell him this is the second time I've rescued Angel. Once more and it's finders keepers.*

TWENTY-ONE

"Wake up, senorita."

Angelina fought against a blanket of darkness that threatened to smother her. Who was calling her? Why?

The persistent voice came again. Someone shook her. "Senorita, it is time for you to wake up."

With a mighty effort Angel opened her eyes. A kindly looking old man with concern written all over his face towered above her. She licked her dry lips. "Wh–who are you? Where am I?" She tried to sit up, but strong yet gentle hands pressed her back against something heavenly soft.

"I'm Doc Brown. You're at the Diamond S."

The Diamond S? What was she doing there? Angel wrinkled her forehead and tried to remember. Oh, yes. She had fled from Papá after he announced his intentions of betrothing her to someone called

Teodoro Menendez. Angel felt a rush of nausea. Her head pounded, and she shrank away from the doctor's touch. "I will not marry him."

If her statement startled Doc Brown, he hid it well. "You won't be marryin' anybody for some time, young lady. What you need is rest. You've been through quite an ordeal. Sheriff Meade's downstairs. As soon as you feel like talkin' about it, he wants to hear what happened." Doc smiled. "Sarah's bringing up a glass of warm milk to help you sleep." He scowled. "No sleeping powders. You've had enough drugs. I hope they hang the dirty varmints who kidnapped you."

The doctor's violent wish helped to clear the fog that swirled in Angel's brain. "Drugs? Kidnapped?"

Doc Brown's jaw dropped. His eyes opened wide. "You don't remember?"

Angel shook her head. "I remember Senor Timothy —" Shame rushed through her. How could she tell the doctor that she had pleaded with Timothy to run away with her and marry her? Or that he had refused? She hastily substituted, "He was going to take me home."

The doctor's faded eyes gleamed. "And then?"

A jumble of thoughts kaleidoscoped through Angel's mind, all too vague to make sense. "You told me I had to wake up."

Doc Brown expelled a great breath. "You remember nothing in between?"

Angel tried hard but failed. "I'm sorry. Is it important?"

He patted her hand. "Right now what's important is that you're safe and need to rest." He smiled as Sarah entered, holding a goblet. "Drink your milk like a good girl, and don't worry about anything. Your daddy is downstairs with the sheriff."

I don't want to see him. Had she spoken aloud? No. Both Sarah and the doctor remained calm. Angel drank her milk and watched them leave. She waited for the click of the latch. It didn't come; the door remained ajar.

"How is she?"

Was that Timothy Sterling's hoarse voice outside her door? Angel struggled to throw off the stupor that slowed her brain and made it impossible to think. Doc Brown's voice floated in to her.

"She's awake, but the last thing she remembers is you saying you'd take her home."

"Nothing else?" Timothy sounded appalled.

"Not until she woke up here." A long pause followed. "It may or may not come back to her," Doc said. "Never can tell. Memory loss often occurs after a bad experience. I'm just an old sawbones, but I figure it's the good Lord's way of helpin' a body get over shock by blockin' it out. Sometimes it's temporary. Other times folks never remember."

"Then I have no proof of what I told the sheriff."

Another long pause. "Sorry, son. I reckon you don't, seein's as how you admitted you didn't recognize the kidnappers."

The despair in Timothy's voice and Doc Brown's flat statement made Angel want to leap from the bed and run to the man she loved. What had happened that was so terrible her mind refused to face it? She closed her eyes and willed herself to find a shred of recollection. None came. Just the same churning in her mind that told her nothing. She racked her brain to no avail. At last the warm milk did its work, and she fell asleep.

Angel didn't learn the story of the kidnapping and her rescue until the next day. Sarah Sterling decked her out in a fluffy white robe and propped pillows behind her back. "You're going to have visitors." Sarah

231

sounded so serious it made Angel wonder. "Doc Brown thinks if you hear what happened it may help to restore your memory. Angelina, it is really important for you to remember." Her voice broke. But before Angel could question her, the doctor, Timothy Sterling, Sheriff Meade, and Papá came in.

"Tim, tell her everything that happened," the doctor ordered. Angel felt a quiver of alarm. He looked as sober as Sarah had sounded.

Timothy grimaced. "Trouble is, I don't know all of it. Last thing I remember is getting whacked on the head. When I woke up, the three men were gone with Ang— uh . . . with Senorita Montoya." He sketched in what had followed. He bore down heavily on the fact that God had directed him to the deserted cabin and made light of his own part in the rescue. Misery shone in his eyes when he finished and turned to her father. "I should have taken better care of her."

Doc Brown snorted. "Don't see how you coulda done any more with a clout to the head that knocked you out cold."

"I agree," Papá said. "I do not understand why my daughter came here alone, but I shall be eternally grateful, senor."

232

Angel cringed. What would he do if he knew the reason she had come to the Diamond S? She bit her tongue to keep from crying out, *Are you grateful enough to Timothy for saving me to allow me to marry him?* She felt a wave of heat creep up from the collar of the bed jacket, but her father's voice broke into her thoughts.

"Does this help you to remember, querida?"

Angel looked from face to face, and a lump grew in her throat. "If only I could!" She clenched her hands. "Why is it so important?"

No one replied.

"Tell me!" She beat her fists against the colorful quilt covering her lower body.

Sheriff Meade scratched his head. "We haven't been able to dig the three fellers responsible outta wherever they've holed up. Even if we do, without your testimony, it's their word against Tim's, and there's three of them."

Butterflies fluttered in Angel's stomach. "You mean they could go free?"

"Something like that," he mumbled. "Say, Doc, I reckon we've been here long enough, right?"

"Right. Out, all of you except her daddy." The crusty old physician waved a dismissive hand. As soon as they left, he turned back to Angel. "Don't worry none about not remembering. Lots of times it just takes something unexpected to trigger off a memory, and everything comes rushing back. By the way, I want you to stay here for at least two more days."

The doctor's statement precipitated a battle royal between him and her father. Doc's mouth turned down, and he obviously lost his patience. "Your daughter stays here. I won't be responsible for what may happen if she's moved. She's had a terrible shock, man; can't you see that?"

Papá didn't give an inch. "All the more reason for her to be in her own home. I am her father and —"

"And I'm her doctor. That settles it."

To Angel's amazement, Papá spread his hands wide and gave in. "Very well. I assume you will tell me when I may take her to La Casa del Sol?"

"You can bet your bottom dollar on that." Some of the fierceness went out of the doctor's lined face, and he grinned at Angel. "You'll be fine, but I'm not taking any chances." He marched out, leaving Angel wanting to laugh at the disgruntled expression on her father's face.

"The House of the Sun is a house of

desolation without you," he said.

Angel sat bolt upright. "Then why do you keep wanting to send me away?" she cried before she could check her words. "First Senor Chavez and now this Senor Menendez. Why must I be parceled off to a man I do not love?" She fell back against the pillows, too weary to say more.

Dark color flooded her father's face. A muscle in his cheek twitched, but he only said, "We shall not speak of this now." He leaned over and kissed her forehead. "Sleep well, my little Carmencita." He walked out, leaving Angelina bewildered. Why had he called her by her mother's name instead of her own? Was Papá weakening?

"May it be so, Jesús." Angel closed her eyes, but she could not shut out the closed look on Sheriff Meade's face just before he left. Or the urgency in Sarah's voice. An alarm bell rang deep in her soul. She added, "And por favor, help me to remember."

Doc Brown was as good as his word. Two days later he gave permission for Angel to go home. She returned to tearful greetings and a warm welcome from all at La Casa del Sol, but her heart yearned for the Diamond S and for Timothy. She also dreaded further conflict with her father.

A day passed. Another. Still he said nothing of Teodoro Menendez. Angel began to breathe easier and hope the young man had gone elsewhere to seek a bride.

A visit from Doc Brown brought news that all of Madera considered Timothy Sterling a hero for rescuing Angel. It filled her heart with joy. Once again she sang while she carried out her duties as mistress of the hacienda.

Her song died less than a week later. Late one afternoon, the butler ushered Sheriff Meade into the courtyard, where Angel and her father sat enjoying the shade. The look in the sheriff's face brought Angel to her feet with one hand to her throat.

"I have bad news." Meade mopped his face with a dusty bandanna and looked straight at Angelina. "Timothy Sterling has been charged with abducting you."

"Imposible." Papá leaped up. "Such a thing cannot be!"

Angel felt as if part of her heart had been torn away. "Surely you do not believe it?"

"Not until Mercy Hot Springs freezes over!" the sheriff shot back. Deep furrows lined his forehead. "The problem is this." He fished in the pocket of his shirt beneath his silver star and brought out a creased piece of paper.

Angel forgot good manners and snatched it out of his hand. For a moment her vision blurred; then she read the accusing words out loud: "If yore a-lookin fer who tuk the angel ask tim sterling where his hat and bandanna is."

Angel turned toward the sheriff. "What does Timothy say about this?"

"That when he came to after bein' knocked out, his hat and bandanna were gone. Said he wondered about it at the time, then forgot it." He licked his lips. "Yesterday, we rode out to the cabin."

"Well?" Her father's question cracked like a matador's whip.

The lawman groaned. "Found Tim's hat and bandanna. That ain't the worst of it. An anonymous note's flimsy evidence, but three fellers rode in and said they witnessed the kidnapping. There'll have to be a preliminary hearing to see if there's enough evidence for a trial." He turned to Angel and spread out his hands to her. "Senorita, you just gotta remember what really happened. It's all that can save Tim. Town's up in arms with folks choosin' up sides. Most folks are for Tim but not all."

For a single, wild moment Angel wanted to lie, to make up a monstrous story that would save Tim. The idea died a-borning.

In spite of the warm afternoon, she felt chilled. "What will happen if he's found guilty?"

The sheriff's face went chalky. His shoulders drooped. "I reckon we won't talk about that. I just wanted you to know what's happened. Also that I'm pleadin' with the good Lord to bring your memory back. He's gotta do it real quick. The hearing's day after tomorrow."

He turned away, and the echo of his boot heels tolled a death knell in Angel's heart.

TWENTY-TWO

When Timothy Sterling stepped down from the carriage in front of the Madera courthouse, his heart sank. It looked like the whole town and most of the folks from outlying ranches had come to his hearing. Their expressions ranged from smiles of encouragement to doubt and downright hostility.

"Make way, here," Sheriff Meade bawled to the crowd milling about outside the Madera courthouse. "This ain't no circus."

Silence fell over the multitude, and then someone called out, "Hangin's too good fer kidnappers."

Timothy spun on his heel, trying to locate the source of the sneering voice.

"Any more of that kind of talk and I'll clear the streets," the sheriff bellowed. "This is the good old U. S. of A. A man's innocent until proved guilty."

A murmur swept through the crowd. Tim

gritted his teeth. A couple of days ago he'd been the big hero. From the sound of things now, a lot of folks had already tried, convicted, and sentenced him. So be it. Tim flung his head back and marched up the steps, backbone straight as a poker.

Just before Tim stepped inside the front door, a veiled figure detached itself from a tall man's arm and started toward him. A clear voice rose above the renewed clamor of the milling crowd. "Senor Sterling did not kidnap me."

A catcall broke off in the middle. Someone gasped.

Tim rubbed his eyes. "Angel?"

She tore off her veil. Her eyes blazed dark fire. "He is innocent."

"What do you have to say about that, Don Fernando?" someone jeered.

The don's face looked harder than rock. "It is as she says. He would never harm my daughter. Come, querida." He took her arm and pulled her back to one side.

For a second, Tim thought she would refuse. He sent her a look of gratitude and was rewarded by a tremulous smile. It sent Tim's spirit racing toward the skies. With Jesus as his Trailmate and the faith and trust he had seen in Angel's eyes, how could he despair? Comforted, Tim entered the courtroom and took his place at the front next to Sheriff Meade and Harold Pinchot, the finest lawyer in Madera. His family filed in behind them, along with Doc Brown and Red Fallon. Tim could feel their support and knew each of them was praying for him.

The room could not hold all those who had come to the hearing. When every seat was filled amidst growling from those who could not get in, Judge Barry entered. Silver-haired and dignified, he seated himself behind the massive podium on the raised platform and looked at Tim. A lightning glance of sympathy crossed the judge's face then vanished so quickly that Tim couldn't be sure he had seen it. The judge pounded his gavel. "The court will come to order. Be seated."

Silence fell, broken only by the rustle of skirts, the shuffle of boots.

"This is a preliminary hearing, not a trial," the judge began. "We are here only to determine if there is sufficient cause to bind Timothy Sterling over for trial."

A hiss came from the back row.

"Bailiff, take that man out," the judge said. "Any further outbursts and I will clear the courtroom."

Tim rejoiced. He had attended a few trials where the judge lost control and chaos reigned. Judge Barry obviously didn't intend for that to happen.

"What are the charges?" the judge asked.

The prosecutor stood. Lean and cadaverous in a black suit, he looked more like an undertaker than a lawyer. "Timothy Sterling is charged with the abduction of one Angelina Carmencita Olivera Montoya." He rolled the name out as if savoring every syllable. Tim wanted to sock him.

Judge Barry's brows drew together. "Is the young lady accusing Timothy?"

The prosecutor stroked his chin with a bony finger. "No. Senorita Montoya cannot remember what happened."

A ripple ran through the courtroom. Judge Barry glared and banged the desk with his gavel. "Then who made the accusation?"

"Sheriff Meade got an anonymous message."

The judge glowered. "That's your evidence? An anonymous message?"

The prosecutor puffed up like a wet hen ruffling her feathers. "It's enough for the state to feel there may be a case against Sterling. Besides, I have three eyewitnesses who will swear they saw Sterling kidnap the senorita. And" — he held up Tim's hat and neckerchief — "these were found in the old homesteader's cabin."

Tim's body jerked. Only Sheriff Meade's iron grip on his arm kept him from leaping to his feet and proclaiming the so-called witnesses bald-faced liars.

The judge appeared taken aback. He fitted the tips of his fingers together and stared at the prosecutor for what seemed like an eternity to Tim. At last he said, "Very well. We will hear your first witness."

After her own ringing endorsement of Timothy's innocence and her father's statement of belief, Angel followed her father into the courtroom. He ushered her to a seat about halfway back, a spot that gave her a clear view of Timothy and the sheriff. She laid her hand on his arm and whispered, "Gracias, Papá."

He patted her hand and smiled. "I only said what I believe." The smile faded. "I just hope . . ."

The *thud* of Judge Barry's gavel cut him off, but Angel's heart throbbed with alarm at the doubt in his voice. Did he fear, as she did, that the discovery of Timothy's hat and bandanna would be incontrovertible evidence? A quick prayer for help from her new source of strength calmed Angel. She leaned forward to better hear every word.

"I have three eyewitnesses who will swear

they saw Sterling kidnap the senorita."

Three witnesses. Three masked riders.
Angel gasped and clutched at the memory.
Nerves atingle, she struggled to remember
more but failed. Yet a crack of light had
pierced the curtain of darkness surrounding
that awful day. She watched the first witness swagger to the front of the courtroom,
straining to see if anything about him
looked familiar.

"State your name," the judge ordered.

The gaudily clad cowhand leered. "Folks
call me Buck, that is, when they ain't callin'
me somethin' worse."

Down went the judge's gavel. *Bang.* "You
will confine yourself to the questions asked.
Bailiff, swear him in."

"Place your right hand on the Bible," the
bailiff ordered. Buck obeyed. "Do you swear
to tell the truth, the whole truth, and nothing but the truth, so help you God?"

"Sure. That's what I'm here fer."

Tim's lawyer sprang to his feet. "Objection! This man is making a mockery of this
hearing."

Bang went the judge's gavel. "Objection
sustained. I'm not warning you again," he
barked to Buck. "One more time and I'll
hold you in contempt of court."

Angel felt a spurt of hope and wanted to

244

cheer. Judge Barry obviously wouldn't put up with nonsense. Would he be able to see through what she knew in her heart were trumped-up charges against Tim?

The prosecutor stepped forward. "Tell us what you know about this matter, Buck. In your own words, just as you told me."

Buck appeared to be in his glory when he said, "It was like this. Me an' two other fellers were headin' fer the Diamond S. We'd heard tell they might be hirin'. It was gettin' on in the day when we come up on Sterling there yankin' the lady off a big white horse. He plumb knocked her out an' threw her on his own horse, a blue roan. Then he mounted an' rode off with her."

Liar! Angel wanted to scream. Her memory flickered and steadied, filling her with horror. Timothy jumping off Blue. A man hitting him with a pistol. Tim lying as if dead. The man hauling her off Blanca. A cloth over her nose and mouth. A slightly sweet odor. Struggling against iron hands. Trying to breathe. Then darkness and waking up at the Diamond S.

Angel leaned close to her father and whispered in his ear. "I remember what happened. What should I do?"

His strong hand clasped her own. "Wait."

On fire to challenge Buck, she forced

245

herself to obey.

He continued. "Now me an' my pards couldn't stand fer that sort of thing, so we follered."

Judge Barry snorted. "Good Samaritans, huh?"

Buck looked puzzled. "Don't know none of those fellers, but we figgered if we took the pretty gal home maybe her daddy'd give us a ree-ward." He looked so pleased with himself that Angel wanted to strike him. "Anyways, we got to the cabin, intendin' to get the drop on Sterling." His face twisted. "He was lyin' in wait. Threatened to shoot us if we made a move. Ran off our horses. It took most of the next mornin' to round them up." His thin lips stretched in a smile.

"He made one bad mistake, though. He fergot his hat and bandanna. Sheriff found them at the cabin."

Judge Barry stopped the recital. "If what you say is true, how come Sterling brought Senorita Montoya back to the Diamond S?"

For the first time Buck looked uncertain. "Uh, I guess he —"

"I object to that question, Judge." The prosecutor cut in. "It calls for a conclusion on the part of the witness."

"Pipe down," the judge said. "I'm just curious to get his opinion. Besides, this is a hearing, remember? Not a trial." He shot the prosecutor a triumphant grin. "And I'm the judge. Answer the question, Buck."

Angel held her breath.

Buck squirmed. "He was prob'ly gonna ask fer ransom, then chickened out when he saw we knew what he was up to."

Sheriff Meade stood. "Beggin' your pardon, Judge, but how about lettin' Tim talk?"

"He will get his turn. Prosecutor, call your next witness."

Buck stumbled out after a venomous look at the judge. The second and third witnesses told the same story almost word for word. Angel noticed that Judge Barry hid his mouth behind his hand a few times. Was it to hide laughter? Disgust?

When the third man finished, Papá stood. "Judge, my daughter has remembered what happened. May she come forward?"

A broad smile crossed the judge's face. "By all means. Swear her in, Bailiff."

Angel's heart thumped when she took the oath. She concentrated on the judge and told her story straight to him.

"That's mighty fine," Judge Barry praised. "Bailiff, bring all three witnesses back into the courtroom." When they came inside, he motioned them to stand before Angel. "Senorita Montoya, you have cleared Timothy of all charges. Now I want you to do one more thing for me. Look at each of these men. Is there anything about them, anything at all, to make you think *they* might be the kidnappers?"

A terrifying moment. Even though all three men had lied, Angel dared not accuse them of kidnapping. What if her testimony sent innocent men to prison? "I don't know. They wore masks."

Still, doubt nibbled at the edge of her brain. There *had* been something, but what? She allowed her gaze to travel from the top of the third witness's head down to his worn boots. Nothing sparked. She did the same for witness number two. Again, no sign of recognition.

Last of all she turned her gaze toward Buck. She closed her eyes. Were those burning eyes the ones she had seen when the rider on the ground brutally struck Tim with his pistol then kicked him in the ribs? *Please, Jesús, help me to remember.* Angel's gaze swept downward. She stared at Buck's fancy boots. Boots with curiously wrought metal strips across the toes.

Angel hurtled from her chair and pointed an accusing finger at him. Her cry rang throughout the courtroom. "It was you! I recognize your boots!"

Buck's face whitened. A look of fear darkened his eyes. With a wild cry, he turned and ran, followed by his fellow witnesses.

"Stop them," Judge Barry shouted. A dozen men, including Papá, leaped after the fleeing men and caught them before they could escape. "Order! Order!" The judge banged his gavel again and again.

But the sound could not equal the hammering of Angel Montoya's heart when she looked at the transfixed face of Timothy Sterling.

TWENTY-THREE

When the Sterlings and Montoyas came out
of the courthouse, the fickle crowd swarmed
around them. Angel couldn't help contrast-
ing their expressions with the doubt many
of them had worn earlier. The need to get
away nearly overwhelmed her. "Take me
home, Papá," she pleaded.

"Sí, but first there is someone I must see."
He helped her into the carriage and turned
toward Red Fallon, who stood nearby, hat
in hand and wearing a broad smile. "Senor,
would you do my daughter and me the
honor of coming to La Casa del Sol before
going to your home? I wish to speak with
you."

Red looked surprised but agreed. "I'll
come as soon as I see Timothy."

Her father nodded and climbed into the
carriage.

What does Papá want with Senor Fallon?
Angel wondered. She was too tired to puzzle

it out. Her eyes closed, and she didn't wake until they reached the hacienda.

"Our guest will be here soon," Papá said. "Perhaps you wish to refresh yourself before he arrives." He helped her out of the carriage.

"Sí. I will hurry." Angel went to her room, splashed cold water on her face, and changed into a soft white gown. A peek from her window showed her father and Red Fallon seated in the courtyard. Angel ran back down downstairs, filled with curiosity.

The men rose when she stepped into the courtyard and waited until she was seated before resuming their places. Her father's impassive face gave no hint as to why he had summoned Senor Fallon. He reached inside his shirt and removed Red's Bible. "I thank you for lending me this, but I no longer have need for it."

Despair clawed at Angel's heart. She saw the disappointment in Fallon's face when he placed the Bible on a small table next to them and asked, "Did you read it?"

"I did." Papá folded his arms.

Angel's hopes for her father finding peace crashed. Her hopes that he would ever permit her to marry Timothy Sterling followed.

"And?"

"Those closest to Jesús did not just follow the law. They walked and talked with Him as *amigos.*" He leaned forward. His eyes glistened.

Angel swallowed hard. Her hands trembled. Was this the answer to her prayers?

Her father's face twisted. "I thought I would die from pain during the long hours when Angelina was missing. As dawn came I promised Dios that if He would save her I would invite Jesús into my heart."

Joy exploded in Angel's soul, but Red cut it short by leaping to his feet.

"No, senor! God wants no strings attached when we come to Him."

"Wait." Her father rose and laid one hand on Fallon's shoulder. "The moment I made the promise I knew I could not bargain with God. I thought of all you had said, of what I had found in your Bible, of the peace I saw that Angelina had found. Then I fell to my knees and told Dios *that no matter what happened* I wanted Jesús to be my Trailmate — as He is yours."

Angel flew from her chair and to her father. "Papá, it is what I have prayed for!"

Red pulled a handkerchief from his pocket and loudly blew his nose. "Senor, even now

252

the angels in heaven are rejoicing with us."

"Sí." Papá wore the same exalted look Angel had seen Timothy, Red Fallon, and the Sierra Songbird wear. The exaltation that lived in her own heart.

He smiled. "For the first time since my Carmencita died, peace came to me. It helped me live through the hours until I received word Angelina was at the Diamond S. It has been with me ever since. I have been able to forgive Dios for taking Carmencita and my son. I still do not understand why, but as Senora Fallon, said, our losses help us to know how God must have felt when He saw His Son crucified."

Papá fell silent then added, "I will always be grateful for the teachings of my childhood. Now I also have something more: a personal relationship with *Jesucristo.* I only regret that I did not listen when Dios first sent you to me, Senor Fallon."

Red shook his head. "You weren't ready to accept what He has to offer." He picked up his Bible. "Are you sure you don't want to keep this?"

"I shall purchase one of my own. And one for Angelina. We will wish to write beside the verses, as you have."

The men shook hands and went out. A few minutes later, Angel heard her father

253

call, "¡Vaya con Dios!" and Red reply, "May the peace of God be with you." The sound of hoofbeats dwindled, but joy and gratitude continued to drum in Angel's heart.

For the next few days, harmony reigned at the House of the Sun. Papá spent less time out on the range and more with Angel. They rode together, laughed together, and shared their newfound joy. Yet he never asked why she had gone alone to the Diamond S. A dozen times she wished to confess but shut her lips.

Neither did she ask about Teodoro Menendez. One of Tío Miguel's favorite expressions when Tía Guadalupe interfered in others' business was, "Let sleeping dogs lie." Angel knew it meant to not stir up trouble. So as the days went by with no further word concerning the would-be suitor, Angel heaved a sigh of relief and said nothing.

Angel also studiously avoided the subject of Timothy Sterling. She often felt as if she was in a period of waiting. Or was it the calm before another storm? Yet Tim's promise clamored for attention:

"I will do the honorable thing and take you home. I shall face Don Fernando like a man and ask permission to call on you. I will tell him I love you the way he loved your mother."

know I'm not your son?"

"You *are* my son, just as much as if Gus Stoddard had never existed."

Tim brushed it aside. "Yeah, but does the don know?"

Matt spread his hand wide. "I can't say. When Sarah and I adopted you and Ellie, it was the talk of the range. But ever since his wife died, Montoya has pretty much kept to himself." Compassion filled Matt's lean face. "I hope it doesn't make a difference, Tim, but you have to make sure he knows."

"Right." Tim blindly turned away. Seeking solitude, he whistled up Blue, saddled him, and rode off into the dusk.

It took Tim a full week of soul-searching and long, lonely rides to find peace and come to the point where he could pray, "Not my will but Yours, Lord."

At last he reined Blue in at La Casa del Sol and slid to the ground. Mustering every drop of courage he possessed, he knocked at the door and asked for Senor Montoya. When the arrogant butler appeared about to refuse, Tim stared him down. His spurs jingled as he followed the servant down the hall and into the courtyard.

"This man wishes to speak with you," the butler announced.

Don Fernando looked up from a jumble of papers and dropped his pencil to the low table where he had been working. "Welcome." He smiled. "You have come just in time to save me from madness. I hate paperwork, but alas, it must be done." He waved for the butler to leave them. "What can I do for you?"

"Permit me to marry your daughter." Tim gulped. It was not what he'd practiced all the way from the Diamond S.

"What?" Don Fernando rose so suddenly the table tipped.

Knowing he'd gone too far to back down Tim said, "I've loved her since I first saw her. I believe she loves me the way your wife loved you."

Don Fernando started to speak, but Tim cut him off. "May I continue, please?" The older man sank back into his chair and motioned Tim to a chair.

Lord, I need help. "Before you speak, there is something you must know." Tim looked Don Fernando straight in the eyes. "Matthew Sterling is not my real father. He and my stepsister, Sarah, adopted Ellie and me years ago. My real father, Gus Stoddard, sold us to Matt, probably the only decent thing he ever did." Tim ignored a slight sound from behind him and continued.

258

"Matt's been wonderful, and I'm a child of my heavenly Father. But I have no honorable earthly ancestors such as you possess."

A rush of flying feet caused Tim to turn. Face flaming, Angel rushed past him and to her father. "Honorable? Papá, except for you, this is the most honorable man I know. When you said I must wed Senor Menendez I begged Timothy to elope with me!"

Don Fernando turned the color of chalk and rose to tower above her. "You asked this cowboy to marry you? You were eloping when you were kidnapped?"

She grabbed his arm. "No! Timothy said he could not do it, even though he loved me. He asked what kind of life we would have should we begin by breaking God's commandment to 'honor thy father and thy mother.' He also said it would break your heart and dishonor you even more than the business with Ramon Chavez."

Don Fernandez looked from her to Tim. "Does she speak the truth?"

"She does. Don't blame her too much, Senor Montoya. She was out of her mind with fear of being forced into a betrothal, or she would never have come to me. If I'd only been able to bring her safely home that day, you would never have needed to know."

Something flickered in Don Fernando's

eyes. A minute passed. Then the don's hand shot out and gripped Tim's. "I have been blind. I thought once Angelina was married she would be happy. I chose men reported to have flawless ancestry and . . ."

Angel laid her hand over his lips. Her voice shook when she asked, "Which is more important, Papá? To marry someone who has such ancestry? Or to marry an honorable man who will be the kind of ancestor to make his children proud?"

Don Fernando staggered as if struck. He fell back into his chair and stared at her. Tim had never seen Angel so beautiful. She stood before her father like a mountain lion protecting her young. Then she knelt beside him.

"Papá, will you not consent to my marrying the one I love, as you did?"

Tim saw the struggle in Don Fernando's face: a war between centuries of tradition and the desire for his beloved daughter's happiness.

Don Fernando slowly stood. He raised Angel to her feet and placed her hand in Tim's. "She is yours. I will arrange for your wedding fiesta." To Tim's amazement, the don's eyes began to twinkle. "I believe this time the right bridegroom will await my Angelina at the altar!" He laughed and strode out.

When the door closed behind him, Timothy placed one finger under Angel's chin and tilted her head back. "Angelina Carmencita Olivera Montoya, how many of those names are you going to keep when we are married?" he asked.

A poignant look crept over her features. "I just want you to call me *wife.*"

Tim caught her close and rested his chin on her shining head. "For as long as we live," he promised — and sealed it with a kiss.

Dear Readers,

When I finished writing *Romance Rides the Range,* book one of my western series, I was planted in spirit on the Diamond S Ranch near Madera, California, in the 1880s. I couldn't bear to say good-bye and move on. It happened again at the end of *Romance Rides the River.*

While writing book three, *Romance at Rainbow's End,* I didn't realize what a deep impression secondary character Timothy Sterling was making on me.

I met Tim again months later while reading the book in published form. Tim's love of mischief, tempered by love and concern for his sister, made me wonder what kind of man he would become. I pictured him planting his booted feet on ground as firm as his faith, cocking his head to one side, and demanding, "Give me the chance to find out."

Romance at the Hacienda is my response to Tim's challenge — and another opportunity for me to visit the Diamond S, its inhabitants, and the gorgeous San Joaquin Valley. It is also the story of a young Spanish senorita who must choose between obeying the commandment "Honor thy father . . ." and claiming her chance for a life of happiness.

May Tim and Angel's struggles to do what they know is right and leave the results to God even in their blackest moments strengthen you in your walk with Him.

God bless you.

Colleen L. Reece

ABOUT THE AUTHOR

Colleen L. Reece was born and raised in a small western Washington logging town. She learned to read by kerosene lamplight and dreamed of someday writing a book. God has multiplied Colleen's "someday" book into more than 140 titles that have sold six million copies. Colleen was twice voted Heartsong Presents' Favorite Author and later inducted into Heartsong's Hall of Fame. Several of her books have appeared on the CBA bestseller list.

The employees of Thorndike Press hope you have enjoyed this Large Print book. All our Thorndike, Wheeler, and Kennebec Large Print titles are designed for easy reading, and all our books are made to last. Other Thorndike Press Large Print books are available at your library, through selected bookstores, or directly from us.

For information about titles, please call:
  (800) 223-1244

or visit our Web site at:
  http://gale.cengage.com/thorndike

To share your comments, please write:
  Publisher
  Thorndike Press
  10 Water St., Suite 310
  Waterville, ME 04901